Mckean County
&
Other Stories

McKean County
& Other Stories

Matt Lang

CLAWFOOT PRESS

Copyright © 2015 Matt Lang
Copyright © 2015 Clawfoot Press

All rights reserved.

No part of this book may be reproduced commerically without permission of the publisher.

Distributed to the trade in the United States by Ingram Spark

ISBN: 978-0-9971080-3-3

First Printing

Manufactured in the United States

Contents

Key West	9
384 Miles to Omaha	27
A Hot Dog Love Story	37
Island Paradise	43
McKean County	51
Stuck	73
Skipping Stones	91
Back To Ur	97
Manila, Mindoro, Manila	107
The Tar Black Road and the Lava Red Moon	135
Six Words, Six Stories	139

*To Mom, Dad, Art, Sue, Gary, Sarah,
and everyone else who helped me grow up.*

Not an easy task, still a work in progress.

Key West

ONE OF Matt Lang's chickens died. A dog got it, tore it up. Matt was brushing his teeth when he heard the squawks and the growls and the flapping wings. He spit in the sink and ran down his back stairs. In the backyard, he found the chicken on its side, under a pear tree, with its entrails pooled in the grass. The chicken's eyes were open and then they weren't. It flapped once, and slid away and was gone just like that.

His daughter was watching from the kitchen window. He didn't think she was ready to see chicken entrails pooled in the grass, so he shouted for her to stay inside until he said she could come out.

Matt dug a hole in the ground, threw the chicken in, and threw dirt on top. He called to his daughter. When she came outside, she asked if the chicken died (yes), if it was in the ground (yes), and if it is was lonely.

A chicken flaps, a chicken scratches, a chicken pecks, and a chicken clucks, but this chicken was doing none of those things. A chicken lives with other chickens, a chicken breaths, a chickens leaves the coop and returns, a chicken knows when the sun comes up and the sun goes down, but this chicken was in the dirt, cut off from the sun and everything else it used to know. That's loneliness. A worse kind of loneliness is being cut off from who you used to be. Death is the loneliest thing because death cuts you off from everything. Matt was standing next to the chicken when it gave that last flap, the feathers and skin and beak all stayed there, but its chickenness, the spark that kept its eyes open, went somewhere else. So the chicken was lonely, but it was lonely even before the feathers and skin and beak got covered in dirt.

THE FIRST TRIP

Check this out: Key West has a law that prohibits the killing of chickens. There's chickens everywhere. They've taken over, dude.

Matt's friend Jody was in the passengers' seat, reading through *The Lonely Planet* guide to The Keys. Well before the chicken and the dog and the yard and the daughter, Matt and Jody took a trip. Jody had just quit his job as a parking garage attendant, a job that he'd held for over three years, a job he took so he could read scripts during the day and audition at night, a job that literally put his ass to sleep, a job that was lonely. He never fit the job, or, really, the job never fit him. From the time he could walk, he felt the world tug at each of his limbs. The world tugged and the booth felt wrapped around his neck. Each day the world tugged a little harder and the booth felt a little smaller, until one day it felt like if he watched one more car come and go and leave him behind he would choke to death. So he got up and walked away, in the middle of the day, on a Wednesday.

He wanted to go to the ocean with Matt Lang because they had been friends since they were five and, though they had gone on many adventures together, Matt Lang had never seen the ocean, a fact that did not sit well with Jody.

How could someone, especially someone with a car and a bank account, not have seen the ocean. It's three-fourths of the globe for fuck's sake?

I grew up poor and my parents didn't love me.

Yeah but since then?

The lingering trauma. Thanks for bringing it up.

They drove south on I-95, stopping only for gas and the bathroom, living on peanuts and beef jerky, singing along to the radio whenever the occasion called for it, and the occasion called for it often because Jody loved to sing and he could sing like God's favorite angel.

They stopped in South Carolina, in the middle of the night. As they set up their tent, as they unrolled their sleeping bags, they could hear the ocean.

Let's hit it, said Jody.
Hit what?
The ocean. Let's swim.
Are we allowed?

They hiked up a dune and from the top, in the light of a half-full moon, Matt Lang saw the ocean for the first time and he was afraid in the way he was afraid the first time a woman reached behind her back to unhook her bra, in the way the ancients were afraid to see the face of God.

Jody was already halfway across the sand, pulling his clothes off as he ran.

THE SECOND TRIP

Six months later, Jody drowned, alone, in that same ocean. He was camping, again, for a week by himself, before he went to New York to meet with the producers of a new travel show for men. Jody was going to be the host, but one night he went swimming and must have found a bad current. His body washed up the next morning, naked and somewhat eaten.

According to Jody's oft-stated wishes, his ashes were divvied up among four friends who were to scatter them in the four directions. Jody could be melodramatic, and his friends loved him for it. Matt took his portion and headed south.

He was going to send Jody back to the ocean, but when he stood again at the top of the dunes of Huntington Beach, he thought the ocean and all its waves looked stupid, like a windup toy continuously walking into a wall. He understood the desire of the ancients to crucify the God that failed them. There was no running this time, only sliding down the dune and walking to the ocean, which was nothing more than a bunch of water and salt that splashed when Matt Lang kicked and punched it.

Exhausted and wet, sitting in the sand, Matt felt ashamed that he'd ever loved the ocean. He'd spent so many years wanting to see it and now he just wanted it to go away, he wanted the tide to roll back over the horizon and show the world everything it had taken. He sat and watched a family play in the waves and he wanted to tell them the truth, that they loved the ocean but the ocean didn't love them. The ocean would just as soon swallow them whole. The ocean didn't deserve Jody. Matt made another plan.

THE FIRST TRIP

After three days in South Carolina, Jody said he was ready to keep going.

Key West. All the way south. Keep going. Don't stop till we hit the end of the road.

Why?

Why the fuck not?

'Cause it's a long fucking way.

It's not that far. We're already like over halfway there, and I don't mind driving.

Jody was taking the tent down as he talked.

THE SECOND TRIP

Matt sat in the sun until he was dry. Even starting from South Carolina, Key West was approximately way the fuck down there, but he decided that that's where he was going to take the ashes. He picked up the bag, hauled himself back over the dune, and walked to his car.

THE FIRST TRIP

Not long after they were clear of the sprawl of Key Largo, Jody pulled the car to the side of the road. There was a small parking area, a little patch of sand, people in the water. Jody turned the car off.

Are we allowed to swim here?

Why the fuck not?

Becau —

But Jody was on his way out the door. Matt stayed in the car and watched him wade into the water, up to his waist.

Jody had been in the water for at least an hour, diving under and coming up, hooting like a cowboy on the open range. There were five other people there. Then three. Then none. When they were alone, Jody pulled off his shorts and threw them to the shore. Matt had moved to the hood of the car and was looking around, nervous, certain they would be caught, and being caught meant, well, something bad, something that would embarrass him, even though he was fully clothed on dry land. He wanted Jody to stop, to get out and to get dressed, but more than that he wanted Jody to never stop, to never dry off, to always be this undressed and free.

THE SECOND TRIP

Key West, with it's many bars and restaurants, had more conch fritters than you could shake a stick at, but Matt Lang was not really in a stick-shaking mood and he didn't like conch fritters, so he didn't order any, not even in Key West, a place called the Conch Republic by those who like to pretend that it's something that it's not.

Matt was looking for a bar he and Jody went to the first time around, but he couldn't remember the name. The Opal Room, The Oval Room, The Orchid House? He knew that it was on Duval

Street, so he thought he'd start on one end and walk to the other. He'd recognize it when he saw it.

On that first trip, they stopped at The Opal Room or The Orchid House and drank bourbon and tequila with a drag queen named Her Majesty and Her Majesty's boyfriend. Encouraged by the tequila and his constitutional need to take every opportunity that came his way, Jody kissed Her Majesty. Her Majesty kissed him back. Her boyfriend punched Jody in the ribs, and Jody bit down on Her Majesty's tongue. Her Majesty slapped Jody and threw a glass of bourbon in his face. Angry words followed, pushes and shoves, before the bartender kicked them all out.

Jody had long since spun that night into an epic narrative, a graphic novel of a tale, a soap opera, a WWE pay-per-view spectacular. It became a set piece. Friends who had heard the story dozens of times would ask to hear it again, knowing each telling would be more grand than the last. For Jody's thirtieth birthday, his friend Eric gave him a series of drawings based on his telling of the tale. Jody had them framed and hung them above his bed.

The ashes would need to go in the bar, somehow.

THE FIRST TRIP

Jody's hair was still a bit wet as he walked a few steps ahead of Matt along Truman towards Duval. The late afternoon was hissing with heat and humidity, and the sun seemed like it lived just above the trees. They had no plan; they only had Jody's guidebook-gleaned knowledge that all the good stuff was on Duval Street. Jody stopped at the intersection, Matt stopped next to him.

Which way?

Jody looked left, Jody looked right. Jody said,

This way.

They both went left and they still had no plan and they smelled like they had been driving for days, which they had. They met a drag queen on the sidewalk. She invited them to a show. Jody took her hand, kissed her fingers, and said they would be delighted. Matt followed him inside.

THE SECOND TRIP

Matt stood in front of The Opal House. He knew it by the name and by the aquarium behind the bar, visible from the sidewalk. Jody's ashes were in the pocket of his shorts. He worked the bag open with his finger but he stayed outside. The bar didn't look right, and he didn't think it was going to look any more right if he went inside. It wasn't the bar from Jody's stories. The bar from Jody's story was gone, swept out to sea. The closest thing left was the set of drawings. The ashes stayed in his pocket and he walked on down the street.

THE FIRST TRIP

On the way back north, just south of Jacksonville, they hit a rainstorm so strong it forced Jody to pull the car over. He put the car in park, put the flashers on, leaned the seat back, said to Matt, Goddamn, this rain's not fucking around.

Matt nodded in agreement. That's some shit.

Jody rubbed his cheek, still sore from the night before. Jesus, it's so fucking loud.

What?

I said the rain is SO FUCKING LOUD!

Then the rain got louder, their world was consumed by pounding water. Matt Lang leaned his seat back, too. They both waited with their hands behind their heads for the rain to let up, which it did before too long. When he could see the highway again, Jody sat his seat up, put the car in drive, and continued north.

THE SECOND TRIP

Mallory Square was crowded, people clustered in four different groups around four different buskers with four different acts involving juggling and balancing. Matt Lang stood and watched a woman on a unicycle juggle knives. He got there late, so he missed her name. What was her name, he wondered? Where did she live? What was her living room like? What kind of soap did she use? Was she happy? Was she lonely? She looked lonely, up there on the unicycle, all by herself, above everybody's heads. He thought about what other questions he might ask her when she came down. Jody would have asked her. Matt put a twenty in her bucket and took a seat on a bench with a view of the sunset.

When the sun goes, man, it goes quick. The sun hangs in the air and looks so big and red and fixed in one place until it reaches that point where you can watch it slide to the horizon like it's sliding down a windshield. Mallory Square buzzed until the sun started to slide. When it started to slide, everyone got quiet and turned to watch.

After the sunset, one by one, the buskers climbed back on their unicycles and resumed their juggling. Couples leaned heads on shoulders. Children played tag. Parents argued against more ice cream. Someone was smoking weed. Matt watched the water get darker and listened to the sounds of life going on.

*

Matt Lang sent his daughter inside to wash up for dinner. He stepped on the dirt that covered the chicken, dragged a flowerpot over the grave, and cried for the first time in years.

After dinner, he helped his daughter brush her teeth and tucked her into bed. He asked her if she wanted to talk about the chicken, but she said no. He kissed her good night and went and sat on his back porch. The sun was going down.

People watch the sun go down, people watch the sun come up, and the sun is never lonely. What if that's how death works?

Matt Lang brushed his teeth and dressed for bed. He got in bed and fell asleep beneath the framed drawings that hung on his wall, his head near the container of ashes that sat on his nightstand.

Illustrations by David Feaman of **defeamanart.com**

The Opal Room

ENCOURAGED BY THE TEQUILA AND HIS CONSTITUTIONAL NEED TO TAKE EVERY OPPORTUNITY THAT CAME HIS WAY, JODY KISSED HER MAJESTY.

"384 Miles to Omaha" was first published in
Pulp Metal Magazine in the Spring of 2014

3 *84 Miles to Omaha*

HE PARKED his truck in front of the Kum & Go in the shadow of the I-80 overpass. There was a station wagon in the lot. He waited. He stared through the signs on the window. Fresh Pizza? It's Time! Two kids made the door chime as they walked out with oversized sodas. They got in the station wagon and the station wagon drove away.

His little girl was going to turn thirteen in two days and she was going to celebrate at home, not in St. Anthony's, Room 722. He missed twelve, missed eleven. He was going to be there for thirteen. He could do this. For her. He could do this for her and it would be okay and she would be happy.

The semis on 80 rumbled above as he stood next to his truck and adjusted his ball cap and sunglasses. The door chimed as he went inside with a gun tucked under his shirt, between his belt and the small of his back. The clerk glanced over the shoulders of a man and woman paying for their coffee and donuts. The man walked to the back of the store and stared at his reflection in the glass door of a cooler filled with flavored water. The sunglasses were too big for his face. He pushed them closer to his face, moved them further toward the end of his nose. Like a kid playing dress up, he thought.

He heard the door chime again as the couple left. Chips, pretzels, and honey-roasted peanuts. He grabbed a package of beef jerky and took it to the checkout. The clerk stood with his back to him, arranging cigarettes on a shelf.

312 miles to Omaha. He doesn't want to stop until he gets there, but the stuff in his guts moves one step closer to the exit and his asshole isn't made of metal. He shifts, trying to keep things where they are. Music would help distract him, but the radio is muffled static.

He wriggles a finger in each ear to see if that will help with the ringing. He feels a tickle and brushes underneath his collar. The way he shakes his hand, it's like he was expecting to find a flower but grabbed an insect. He rolls down his window and sticks his hand out, he spreads his fingers and flicks his wrist but he can't shake it. He knows what it is and wonders what it was: Maybe thoughts of running down a narrow alley? Or the feel of gravel digging into hands and knees after a fall?

He threw the jerky on the counter. One moment, please, the clerk said.

The clerk put the last carton in place. He was taller than the man thought he'd be. The man looked back over his shoulder. Still alone. He pulled the gun and aimed for the center of the clerk's back, but his hands were shaking. The gun was a dog on a leash and the clerk was a squirrel.

237 miles to Omaha. Flashing lights behind him, way back but closing fast. He can't hear sirens for the ringing in his ears, but the lights ride up in the rearview, and there go his guts again, they've pushed the button, called the elevator. He pulls onto the shoulder. The whole cab smells of blood.

He kills the engine, puts both hands on the wheel. He'll surrender without a word; just get him to a fucking toilet. The cop passes. A blinking, rapid ghost.

Down a slight hill, in a field off to the right, he sees an owl fly out the window of an empty barn. The owl flies across the road in front of him and lands on top of a utility pole. The man looks at the owl. The owl looks at the man and cocks its head, puffs its feathers to make itself look bigger.

The clerk turned around and saw the gun, didn't jerk, didn't yell. He put his palms on the counter and looked straight into the gun.

Open the register.

The clerk looked down at him, through him, down into his beating heart.

No.

The man held the gun tighter, pointed it straighter, as if that would prove that he meant what he said.

Look, man, don't try to be a hero.

I am not trying to be a hero, my friend. What is it that you are trying to be?

I don't want no troub —

The clerk cocked his head a notch to the right.

Then why are you pointing a gun at me?
I just came for the money, man.
You cannot have the money.
Shoot him in the arm? In the leg?
I'm gonna count to three and then you're gonna open the register.
Counting until three will not make a difference. You should put the gun away and go home.
Not without the money.
The man fired into the ceiling, knocking his hat askew and his glasses crooked. He jabbed the gun towards the clerk as he straightened the glasses and hat.
Is this the best you can do?
What did you say?
Is this the best you can do? For money, is this the best you can do?
This guy. Who the fuck? The best he could do? He thought of his daughter and her failing lungs, the nights in the hospital, the night his wife walked away, the pipes that burst last winter, the father that can't feed himself, the job he had for fifteen years, the last specialty knife he packaged to be shipped away, the interviews since then, the bundle of nos. Yes, motherfucker. This is the best he could do. What the hell did this guy know? How long had this guy been here? This guy here meant one less job, but fuck it, he was here doing what he needed to do...
What do you care?
My friend, you are not made for this.
The clerk's eyes were fixed like stones in his face, so certain. The clerk was right; the man's mouth was dry and he wasn't breathing. The safety was off, the hammer was back, but he couldn't pull the trigger.
One more ruffle and the owl flies away. The man sees the screen on his phone light up. His ex-wife, probably wondering where he is, why he hasn't picked his daughter up yet. He imagines something more serious, cries of where are you, troubled breathing and his daughter's gasping mouth, but he can't help now. He lets the call go to voicemail

then turns the phone off.

As he does, he smears the screen with the stuff still stuck to his hand. Was it grief for someone who went missing on a walk to get a newspaper, a woman crying at the kitchen table? Cold breakfast on the plate and the smell of eggs lingering inside and clean laundry hanging outside and a wife pouring four cups of tea and a hand cramping around the receiver and the wish that the receiver was the throat of the police officer on the other end, the shine of the frantic spit spattered on the mouthpiece?

219 miles to Omaha. Rest area. He walks toward the bathroom with clenched steps, distracting himself by counting the cars in the parking lot — one, two, three — when a boy bursts through the rest area doors and smacks into him. Pieces of grey and black from his sleeve stick to the front of the boy's shirt: the taste of figs, a brother's face, the smell of an airport.

The boy steps back and holds his arms wide, away from his shirt. The man runs past him. The boy will tell someone, but the man needs to do what he needs to do.

The door chimed. The man flinched. The clerk lunged across the counter and grabbed the gun, pulled the man to the supply side of the counter. The man landed on top of the clerk, heard a crack, felt it in his knee. All hands were on the gun. The clerk tried to bite his face. The man arched and looked away, the clerk spit on his cheek. He kicked his leg, trying to get leverage so he could drive his knee into the clerk's crotch, but his boot couldn't get traction, it drew a scramble of black streaks on the tile.

The clerk's hands were as hard as the gun; the man's hands were losing their grip. The man held his breath; the clerk breathed deep and steady as he twisted the gun and with it the man's fing —

...

He undoes his belt and pulls down his pants but before he makes it to sitting he sprays liquid shit on the wall behind him, on the pipes of the toilet, on the handle that flushes. Shit runs down the back of his thighs into the jeans and underwear gathered at his knees. He grabs handfuls of toilet paper and wipes his legs. He can't sit because the toilet seat is covered with foul clots of shit and chunks of undigested lettuce and tomatoes. He squats and cleans out his asshole as best he can. The smell gags him. He doesn't even try to clean the toilet or walls. He takes his jacket off and his hat and sunglasses and rolls them into a bundle and takes the bundle to the trashcan in the corner and stuffs them and a memory of riding to a safe house down among the fast food wrappers and snot-filled tissues.

He keeps his head bent as he moves down the sidewalk. The ringing in his ears has diminished so he can hear the boy's voice from across the parking lot.

That's him daddy, that's the man.

He gets in the truck and slams the door. The boy's father walks towards the truck, shouting something, but he backs it up and pulls away. He looks in the rearview and sees the man making a phone call. He smells like shit. Dribbles of shit in his pants. Bits and pieces of the clerk are in the patch of chest hair above the buttons of his shirt. There are pieces down the back of his neck, more in the hairs that grow over his wrist. Pieces in his ear, in his hair, in his eyebrows, caught in his teeth, dissolving down the back of his throat, the sound of a child's laughter and a promise to his wife.

217 miles to Omaha, to an old girlfriend who wouldn't ask questions. A warm shower. A cold beer. A bed with clean, dry sheets. He'll call his daughter on her birthday, and make plans to celebrate when he gets back home.

"A Hot Dog Love Story" was first published as Flash Prose in *Atticus Review*: six degrees left of literature, in the Fall of 2013.

A Hot Dog Love Story

BRAD WINSLOW wonders why the father and son sitting in seats 1 and 2 in Row G in Section 512 won't stand, if only half way, so that he could have an easier time getting to seat 7. Why do they remain seated, forcing Brad Winslow to step over their knees and in between their feet? Not only do they not move, but the father also mumbles, "Christ", when Brad Winslow's crotch passes in front of his face, as if Brad Winslow has no claim on seat 7 or the path thereto. Brad Winslow wonders if *the* world is full of jerks or if *his* world is full of jerks. How would he figure that out? Some kind of survey, but how do you quantify a jerk? Surely mumbling "Christ" into the crotch of someone who just wants to get to his seat in time for batting practice qualifies. Right? Brad Winslow (metaphorically) puts the question in his pocket so as to enjoy batting practice (BP) without distraction.

But what's this? Distraction! Distraction is sitting in seat 9 in Row F in Section 512. Brad Winslow (literally, in a small, spiral notebook), takes the following notes about her appearance: strong jaw, eyebrows thicker than the national average, small nose, turned up, a mouth that smiles when she says, "One, please", and cheek bones that tie it all together. If Brad Winslow were the type of guy that noticed the color of someone's eyes, he would see that her eyes are the color of today's sky, which is to say they are high sky blue. But Brad Winslow, for some reason, does not notice the color of people's eyes.

The woman in seat 9 receives the hotdog and gives the vendor the money with the same hand, in the same motion. Brad Winslow has never considered — never even thought to consider — that there might be a right or wrong way to receive a hotdog from a vendor, but now he knows, he has seen with his own eyes, the one perfect way. He scribbles in his notebook, words and diagrams, desperate to understand the exchange and if it could be replicated, and, if so, could be replicated by him, Brad Winslow, and if it could be replicated by him, should it be, or was it a distinctly feminine way to purchase a hotdog? There were answers to these questions, as there were answers to all questions, including the question of how to best apply ketchup and mustard to a hot dog. Answer: the way the woman in seat 9 is applying it right now! Brad Winslow knows he is in the presence of greatness. Brad Winslow is watching the woman in seat 9 eat the hot dog bite by well-chewed bite, each bite taken with consideration, and he can't stop watching. He closes his notebook because he feels dizzy. If she is this good at purchasing and consuming a hot dog, she probably also knows the perfect way to tie a knot in her shoe, and the best place to sit on a bus, and the most effective months of the year in which to get a haircut. Why is she at a baseball game alone? Brad Winslow knows why he is there alone, because he is a friendless thing, but she must know how to make friends. Maybe she is there because she knows what she likes, and she knows how to get it, and two of the things she likes are going to baseball games alone and eating hotdogs while she's there.

The woman in seat 9 does not eat the last bite. Why does she not eat the last bite? Perhaps it is all bun and no dog, perhaps it is overly soggy with condiments, or perhaps she is full and doesn't see the need to eat one bite beyond her satisfaction. Whatever the reason, she wraps the last bite in the wrapper and drops it at her feet. Brad Winslow draws a map in his notebook, X marking the location of the wrapper. For the rest of the game, she doesn't talk, doesn't text, doesn't tweet, and when the game is over she stands up and leaves.

Brad Winslow documents her every move and stays seated until the rest of Section 512 departs to the concourse. Then Brad Winslow drops to his hands and knees, refers to his notebook, locates the wrapper, and removes the uneaten bite. Brad Winslow turns it between his thumb and finger. There is a little bit of dog left in the bun, but no ketchup or mustard. Brad Winslow pops the piece in his mouth and wonders if maybe, just maybe, this is his first taste of love.

"Island Paradise" was first published in *Our Stories* in the Spring of 2010.

Island Paradise

Morning

He must have been here early in the morning while I was still sleeping. He moves without sound, like mist. He rolls in with the tide and then slides back into the wide sea and I would never know he came if it were not for the gifts. Today he left a chicken.

Afternoon

The weather is perfect. It always is, almost tyrannical in its perfection. If it ever rained, I could sit and relax. What would the rain sound like on my roof? I'm always on my feet, it seems. I plow, I plant, I harvest, I tend. I walk to the shore and pause, I do let myself do that, and listen to the waves. They also never rest.

Evening

Three days ago he left a gift — a box — that I have not opened yet. The box is neatly wrapped. He hates to wrap gifts. Strange. He is playing games. He likes the mystery. My baked beans are almost warm. After I eat them, I will open the box.

Late at night

A ukulele? What the fuck?

Morning

I think I heard him late at night, walking up and down the rows of crops. He might have stopped to lean against the pen I built for my goats. They probably ignored him; they usually ignore me. They have all the grass they can eat in their pen. They keep to themselves in their little goat world. They make milk. I sell the milk. A fine arrangement. They don't complain much. Goats are good listeners.

Afternoon

I sleep in the bow of a broken boat. The bow is all that remains of the Floating. We all live on islands now. We all sleep in bows. For so long we floated on the sea in our Own Boats. We could visit each other, and talk, and have boat races, and picnics in which we would tie our Own Boats together and pass food and drink from vessel to vessel. But we always stayed in the boats. Our Own Boats. Then came the Season of Drifting Away.

Evening

I went to visit him. His island is nice, busy but not too crowded. He didn't seem interested in company. He stood off to the side. I stood next to him for a while but we did not speak. He seemed nervous. He blinked a lot and shifted his eyes from side to side. It made me nervous. I blinked a lot, too. What are we doing? We just stood there, blinking, looking up at the sky. As if the answers were in the sky.

Late at night

I leaned the ukulele against my shelter. I can't play, and there is no one to teach me.

Morning

We all washed up on our islands in the Season of Drifting Away. Most of us thought the Floating would end with a big storm, or an unexpected wave, but what happened was we just stopped paying attention to each other. A few of us were lost, then a few more, then more. The races were less spectacular; the floating less impressive. There was less food and drink to pass around. Then most of us were gone. Then we were all gone. No more Floating.

Afternoon

Did he steal some yams? I think he stole some yams. I now have fewer yams.

Evening

I bought an old crate and two barrels. The crate makes a nice table, and you can sit on the barrels. I hope he comes to visit and I hope he stays and sits with me. I have cabbage soup, but it won't stay warm for long.

Late at night

I don't feel in control. I don't make the choices. Someone is moving me.

Very late at night

I am so alone.

Morning

We drifted to separate islands. Our Own Boats were wrecked. We are farmers, all of us. Everyone. We grow crops, tend to animals, we fish and cook. And sell all of it. We get rich quick. It is a kind of miracle: crops grow in hours, trees mature in days. Amazing. But it never stops. It just keeps growing. There are no seasons; there is no rest. Just as quickly as a plant blooms, it dies. It is relentless. Our islands grow bigger, but we can never share them. We can visit, but never stay together. It is a kind of curse.

Afternoon

I asked a goat, "If I pay more attention, will I be allowed to stay?" She gave no answer, but her face was kind. Maybe he wants a goat. Yes, I will give him a goat.

Evening

He came when I was fishing. The nets were in the water and we were standing. I wanted to hold his hand. I wanted to touch. We looked at the ocean. We listened to the birds. In the distance, far in the distance, I heard a sound like a foghorn. It sounded like a long time ago. I thought about the Floating. I wish I had known him then. I would have tied my boat to his, even climbed in his. We would not have drifted apart. We would have stayed. Is that even possible? Did such a thing ever happen? Does anyone, anywhere, have anyone against whom they can warm their feet at night? I moved my toes through the wet sand and tried to touch his. He was gone. He never said a word. I pulled in my nets. Empty. The fish had escaped.

Late at night

I would give him all my yams, if he would only ask.

"McKean County" first appeared in *The Rusty Nail Literary Magazine* in the Summer of 2015.

McKean County

McKean County, Pennsylvania is located in the Allegheny Mountains, three hundred miles north of Pittsburgh, ninety miles south of Buffalo, New York, and twenty-five years behind anywhere else. Matt Lang grew up there and moved away. He lives in Chicago now.

Matt Lang & Wayne Strohman
decide to go to a bar

On his most recent trip home to McKean County, Matt Lang learned that many women in the area were getting their breasts done. Wayne Strohman shared the news over bacon, eggs and coffee at Marcy's Diner in Derrick City.

Anyone I know?

Stephanie Knight.

Have you seen her?

Last night. Figured I'd stop by the Eagle, have a drink, see who was there, and there she was with two new tits.

Matt nodded.

And?

I asked if I could see them and she said no. Tobacco juice spilled from his mouth. He wiped it with his sleeve. Fuckin A? I was like, what's the point of getting em done if you're not gonna share?

Wondering if it wasn't because Wayne was probably dribbling tobacco juice down his chin even then, Matt took a ten out of his wallet.

Well, keep at it. She'll come around.

Matt threw the bill on the counter.

Oh, I will, and she will if I can get her drunk enough.

Nice catching up, Wayne.

Got another? Ten?

Matt threw another on the counter and put on his coat. Wayne put on his.

Goin out to the Eagle again tonight. Guaran-damn-ty Stephanie will be there.

The divorce isn't final, dude.

Yeah? And?

As often happened during a conversation with Wayne, Matt didn't quite know what to say.

Matt went with Wayne to the Eagle that night. He had not been to the Eagle in ten years, more than ten years. It, like most everything else in McKean County, looked the same. There was the deer head over the door, there was the Earnhardt poster on the wall, there was the reminder that The West Was Not Won With a Registered Gun above the tap which offered the same three beers: Bud, Bud Light, Yuengling.

Matt ordered a Yuengling from the same bartender, Dora, who looked like she had aged two years for every one lived. Wayne ordered a Bud.

They sat at a booth in the corner. Stephanie Taylor walked in with a much younger man who Matt recognized but couldn't name. They didn't see Matt or Wayne and took seats at the bar with their backs to them.

That's the other thing: Gettin their tits done *and* datin guys at least ten year younger than em.

Who's that?

Ryan Reevus. His brother was in my class.

Jesus, can he even drink?

Oh, yeah. He's like twenty-five or twenty-six. Not that Dora gives a shit, of course.

Of course.

Stephanie leaned on the bar and slid her ass back. Matt looked at it, there, on the stool, perched, as he finished his beer. Wayne finished his beer and went to work on a wad of chewing tobacco, using his glass as a spittoon.

Why didn't you ever hit that?

I tried, man.

No, you didn't try, you fuckin pussed out. Did you ever ask her? No, didn't think so.

Wayne spit, wiped his mouth with the back of his hand and leaned in.

First you ask to see their tits. Then you ask to see their twat. Then you say, we've come this far, we might as well fuck.

That's how you do it, huh?

Yes, that's how you do it. It's not fuckin rocket science. Let's put it this way: There's five women in this bar right now, right? I've fucked four of them.

Matt counted.

So you fucked everyone here but Dora?

No, I fucked Dora. Best fuckin head I ever got.

Matt finished his beer.

So -

Stephanie never let me fuck her.

See, it's not that easy.

Yeah, but I'm a fuckin fat ass. And at least I tried.

MATT LANG & STEPHANIE TAYLOR: A BRIEF HISTORY

1.

Matt Lang first saw Stephanie Taylor in the hallway on the first day of school of seventh grade. His locker was across the hall from hers. He noticed her bangs first, then saw her eyes, and below her eyes, a

smile that made it hard for him to sleep at night.
   Her tits weren't there yet, not really, but by the time they showed up in eighth grade, Stephanie had replaced *Vogue* era Madonna as the most frequent guest star in Matt's masturbatory scenarios. His infatuation lasted until their senior year, when it was undone in two parts.

A.

Stephanie walked into homeroom and took her seat. She looked upset. Matt leaned forward and asked her what was wrong.
   Todd and I broke up.

i.

On January 17th, 1991, Todd Parnell, in the bleachers of Otto-Eldred Jr.-Sr. High School, during the third quarter of a basketball game between the Otto-Eldred Terrors and the Coudersport Falcons, gave Matt Lang a titty twister so vicious that it drew blood. The reason for this: Matt was wearing a *faggot shirt*, a *faggot shirt* being, in the estimation of Todd Parnell, a shirt with buttons.

ii.

Matt wanted to jump up and throw his desk through the window, so unbridled was his joy. Instead, he reached out, put his hand on her shoulder, and lied,
   Jesus, that sucks. What happened?
   He's a total asshole is what happened.
   Matt wanted to say, What tipped you off: the fact that he shoots road signs for fun? That, at the age of twenty-one, he still thinks it's something to belch as loud as possible? That he wears a Confederate flag ball cap, plays *Gimme That Nut* from his 1987 F250 at a volume that rattles windows, but sees not the

contradiction? That he hits you sometimes?

I'm sorry.

Well, I'm not. Fucking asshole.

Matt sat back in his seat and planned their first date.

B.

Two weeks later, Stephanie walked into homeroom and took her seat. She was smiling. Matt leaned forward and noted that she looked happy.

I am. Todd and I are back together. We had a great talk last night and then had great sex.

Matt wanted to jump up and throw his desk through the window, so complete was his rage. Instead, he reached out, put his hand on her shoulder, and lied.

Great. That's great.

He'd planned to drive her over the hill into Olean to see a movie. On the way, she was going to talk and clear her head, and he was going listen because he was good at that. He was going to tell her about all the good things she deserved. He was going to make her laugh. After the movie, he was going to take her to Renna's where they were going to each get a slice of pizza and he was going to reach across the table with a napkin to wipe the little bits of cheese and sauce from her chin, and, since he'd gone that far anyway, he was going to kiss her mouth.

Instead, Matt sat back in his seat and practiced regarding Stephanie with indifference.

II.

He saw her during his sophomore year of college, on the sidewalk in front of the video store in Eldred. He was home for winter break; she was home because she never left. It was night and the snowflakes were falling so slowly, as if they were being lowered on fishing line.

He didn't recognize her right away because she'd straightened her hair. She felt dumb. She hated the change.
    I got it done a few weeks ago.
    It looks nice.
    She looked at the sidewalk.
    Thanks.
    She looked at the plastic bag he was holding.
    What movie?
    He tried to think of a lie and failed.
    Barb Wire.
    With Pamela —
    Yeah.
    Oh.
    Now he looked at the sidewalk.
    How long are you home for?
    About two more weeks.
    Maybe I'll see you?
    He did not see her, but when he came home that summer he heard from Wayne that she was pregnant and engaged to Todd Parnell.

Matt Lang Talks to Stephanie Taylor for the First Time in Many Years

Looking at Stephanie on the barstool, he did not feel indifferent. He wanted to talk to her. He walked to the bar and stood next to her left shoulder. She didn't look at him. He ordered another beer and pretended he'd just noticed her.
    Is that Stephanie Taylor?
    She turned, her face went long with surprise, Well if it isn't Matt Lang.

He took a seat on the barstool next to her. It is, it is. How the hell are you?

I'm good. How are you? Still in Chicago?

Still in Chicago.

They were there, obvious, hovering at the bottom of his field of vision, and he didn't want to be that guy, that guy that just ogled breasts, so he stared at the shine on her teeth. But he was curious, and he looked when she leaned back to introduce him to Reevus. Ridiculous snow globes in a teal, v-neck, sweater.

Reevus ashed his cigarette, and took Matt's outstretched hand, which felt the gravitational pull of the oversized tits. Reevus gave a wordless nod, pumped Matt's hand once, and then resumed smoking and staring straight ahead.

How long are you around for?

As Stephanie spoke her face aged to match the skin of her neck. It looked twenty years older than her tits and was colored with the unearthly darkness of too many trips to the tanning salon. The discrepancy intrigued Matt. In the instant between when she finished her question and he gave his reply, he calculated that if he slept with her it would be like sleeping with a woman who was older than, younger than, and the same age as him.

A few days. I fly back Sunday morning. I've been here since Wednesday.

Are you by yourself? Don't you have a kid?

The kid is with her mom and her folks in Ohio.

They paused for beer drinking. She looked over the top of the glass and let her eyes drift down Matt's body, the shoulders and chest that filled out his shirt, the stomach that, unlike the stomachs of other men at the bar, didn't drape over his belt buckle.

Sorry I don't get to meet her.

My ex? I don't think you'd get along.

She gave him a little backhand slap on his shoulder.

I meant your kid, silly.

Oh, yeah. Next time.

It was time to take a long drink of his beer. It was getting warm because the glass was unnecessarily close to his chest.

You have kids, too, right?

Her glass empty, she stretched her arms out in front of her, over the bar, and rounded her back like a cat.

Yeah, a son and a daughter.

How old are they?

She straightened up.

He's twelve and she's ten.

So, what, seventh grade and fifth grade?

Yep. Can you believe it?

Matt Lang shook his head and laughed through his nose and took another drink.

Reevus left the bar and went to play pool with a group of guys Matt assumed were his friends. Stephanie turned her head back and forth as if working out a krick in her neck. They were silent. The jukebox played *More Human Than Human* and Wayne replaced Reevus.

Hey, told ya she had some big ol titties. You gonna let *him* touch em?

I'd let him before I let you, pervert.

Deep down in a hidden and shameful corner of his soul, Matt became excited.

Ya hear that, Lang?

But he wouldn't because he's a gentleman, unlike some people.

Bullshit. Tell her, Lang. Tell her you would. Tell her that's bullshit.

Deep down in that same hidden and shameful corner, he knew that it was bullshit.

Wayne, you're interrupting.

Hey, I'm just tryin to help out here. You know he's a writer, right? He'll be all sensitive and insightful and shit.

You wanna help? Buy the next round.

Okay, but promise me you'll at least *try* to touch em.

Stephanie turned to face Matt, removing Wayne from the remainder of the conversation.

You're a writer?

Kind of. Not really. I'm trying. When I get a chance.

I remember you wrote some really good stuff in high school.

Matt scratched his forehead and wondered why that statement made his stomach drop so.

Thanks, I — Thanks.

They ordered two more beers. They talked more as they drank them. She looked at him with a tilted head. He matched her tilt. She smiled.

I think you should do something with me.

He looked over her ear toward the pool table.

What about —

He has to work tomorrow night. Come get me anytime after three.

He chewed a bit on his bottom lip.

Okay. After three.

She left with Reevus after that round of beers. Wayne had left with the first willing female, a woman Matt did not recognize, possibly because she'd graduated in the 70's. That left Matt alone at the bar. He did not want even one night of his singular life on this earth to end with him sitting at the Eagle until closing time, so he paid his bill and walked out the door. He crossed a set of train tracks and walked to a small park and found a bench. He was too drunk to drive home, drunk enough to not mind the cold. He sat with his back to the tracks and looked over the park. It was quiet and dark in ways that Chicago never could be. He slouched and closed his eyes, thought maybe he could feel the stars twinkle against his face. The bench was hard and the air was cold, and the combination made him shiver. It also made him have to piss.

There was a sturdy maple waiting for him in a stand of trees that separated the park from the Allegheny River. He opened his zipper and extracted his shriveled dick. He watched his piss splatter and steam, and considered the nature of the breast job: Was it fact or fiction? On which shelf should it be shelved? Was Stephanie writing a memoir or a novel? The implants were fake, yes, but they were under *her* skin, and therefore part of *her* body, and her body was real, was true, so were they now part of the truth of her body? Do embedded lies become part of that whole truth? Or was the whole truth now spoiled, and every part with it? Was her hair a lie? Were here eyes lies? Was that smile now a lie? Or did the fiction point to a truth that was even *more* true?

He shook off, told himself to remember this; it would make for a fine piece of writing. He had piss on his hand. He wiped it on the side of his jeans.

Matt walked back toward the bench and saw someone lurching along the tracks, looking like they might fall over at any moment. Someone else, he thought, too drunk and too far from home.

MATT LANG & STEPHANIE TAYLOR
GO ON A DATE

Matt pulled up to Stephanie's house in his mom's car. It had been twelve, fifteen years since he'd driven down this street. The houses looked thirty-percent more ramshackle. More boards on windows, more cars on blocks in driveways, more awnings propped up by two-by-fours. He couldn't bring himself to get out of the car and admit he was part of this world. He watched while Stephanie came down her front steps carrying a canvas duffle bag. She threw the bag in the back seat where it landed with a thud and a clang.

Hey.
That mouth.
Hey. I thought we could head to Olean, get something to eat.
She sat down, pulled the door closed.
What's with the bag?
She clicked her seatbelt in place. Nosey much?
Just curious.
Let's go. I'm up for anything.

As he drove down her street, he rummaged through his archive, over two decades old, of things he'd imagined about Stephanie. He pulled out Conversations That Might Somehow Lead To Us Having Sex. He always imagined such a conversation would take place in a car, with him driving, and would include her somehow indicating that she was up for anything.

On the way out of town, he saw a house surrounded by police tape.
Shit, what happened there?
She scratched the spot between her eyebrows. I don't know. We heard sirens at around two-thirty. My dad went out to try to see what was going on, but the police had everything blocked.
Who lives there?
It's been empty since Mrs. Randell died, but our neighbor said they took three bodies away in an ambulance.

He assumed it was meth-related, that they'd been using the house as a meth lab. He assumed they had cooked their product wrong and poisoned themselves. He assumed they used their dying breaths to try to call 911. He assumed they dialed the wrong number. He did not have a high opinion of most people in the area.

He thought about sharing this theory with Stephanie, but hesitated because Conversations That Might Lead To Sex did not include crystal meth. On the other hand, he was probably right, because he pays attention, and if he could show Stephanie that he pays attention, even if the demonstration came in the form of an observation about the activities of drug addicts in McKean County, well —

Probably a bunch of meth heads that fucked up their last batch.

That's what my dad thinks. That's actually almost exactly what he said, word for word.

They were driving through the swampy floodplain of the Allegheny River. Bare and dying trees were lined up on either side of them. In the light of the low evening sun they looked like a starving horde, waiting for Matt and Stephanie to leave the road so they could catch them in their branches, drag them into the stagnant water, and feed on them far from the ears of any other people. But Stephanie wasn't thinking about the trees. In fact, she shifted in her seat and angled her body towards Matt.

Maybe you should take this next left.

Eldred was behind them, and there was only one more driveway, one more building before miles and miles of trees.

This one? By the VFW?

She raised her eyebrows and bit her lip. He felt a shift in his pants. By The VFW was a place he had never been, but it fit the imagined scenario. Most everyone else in his graduating class had gone by the VFW to get or give their first blowjob, and many blowjobs thereafter.

The VFW was built for this. There was just one way in and one way out, a narrow gravel driveway, with swamp and trees in every other direction. On the backside of the building, they would be invisible from the road. No other vehicles, no other people would happen to pass by. No one would see, no one would hear, anything that happened there. Furthermore, for what did those veterans of foreign wars risk everything, for what did they sacrifice so much, for what did they spill blood and have their blood spilled, if not for this very freedom? The freedom of assembly, of expression, the freedom to communion with one's gods at the time and place of one's choosing.

He turned left. She directed him to the appropriate parking spot.

She rubbed him through his jeans. He kissed her and took off her jacket. She opened his zipper and took out his cock. He worked his hands up her shirt and under her bra. She bent over and put his cock in her mouth. He took his hands on a trip around each breast. They felt like water balloons filled with wet sand. They felt untrue. At the same time, he wanted to see them. So he asked.

Can I see them?

She lifted her shirt over her head and unclipped her bra. They were steadfast, nary a jiggle. His eyes floated up to her face. He tucked his dick back in and zipped himself back up. She looked embarrassed, like she was all too aware of their absurdity, and self-conscious about Matt's awareness of her embarrassment.

Do you like them?

Yeah, I mean, I've always liked them. I liked them before. I mean, I've liked you a long time.

Stephanie was looking somewhere off to the right, through the windshield.

I know.

Matt put both his hands on the steering wheel. Stephanie put her shirt back on.

Stephanie, can I ask why?

She looked at the dashboard. I wanted something just for me. I spent two years taking care of my mom, and taking care of my kids, and working. My mom fought so hard. She wouldn't let go. I loved her fight but it wore me out. After she died, I felt like an old lady, like I was falling apart. I wasn't ready for that.

She pinched the skin between her eyes and thought more thoughts that she didn't say out loud. And I thought they'd be fun. I thought it would be something different.

Matt shifted. No, I mean, why this? Why go out with me tonight?

Stephanie shifted. Oh. Same reasons, I guess. She turned toward him and leaned against her seat. What about you?

I saw you in the bar and you looked beautiful. We started talking and my stomach dropped.

Stephanie let a tear roll down her face and fall off her chin. She pulled him in and she kissed him with her mouth open, jaw firm but responsive. She wouldn't have kissed him like that in high school. She leaned the seat back. He moved over her. She took off her shirt again. Everything looked just right. Now he asked, Do *you* like them?

I do.

He kissed her mouth, her neck, between her breasts. A shadow passed behind the car. Matt sat up.

Did you see that?

Stephanie sat up.

No, what?

Someone's here.

As soon as he said the words, Matt knew it was Wayne come to fuck with them. He was about to curse Wayne's name when he heard what sounded like a dead trout smacking against his window. He turned and saw Wayne, clawing at the handle, trying to open the door, wearing the same clothes as the night before, and missing half his face.

Matt screamed, turned the key, and the engine growled to life. He put the car in reverse and stomped the peddle to the floor. Wayne spun to the ground.

What the fuck?

Then there's this.

Stephanie turned to the backseat and brought the duffel to her lap; Matt whipped his head forward and back, trying to understand. There were more people in the parking lot. Did they do that to Wayne? My God, he left Wayne! Should he go back for Wayne?

Wayne, we should, what's happening?

Matt sent gravel flying as he spun the car around. The sun was setting, but he could see three, four, five other people in the parking

lot. They all looked drunk, and were all moving toward the car.
	Zombies.
	The driveway to the road was blocked. Matt looked left, right, left, right trying to think of a way out.
	Zombies?
	They showed up about five or six years ago. You ask five people where they came from, you'll get five different answers, but everyone will tell you they came from somewhere else. No one wants to admit that they came from right under our feet.
	Matt sized up the group of zombies. Wayne and the woman he left the bar with. Dora and one of Reevus's friends, a squirrelly little motherfucker with the mustache of a seventeen-year-old. He aimed for him and floored it.
	The duffle rattled and clanked as Stephanie rummaged through it. There's never been that many of them, only ever a handful shuffling around at any one time. Enough to make more, not so many that we get overrun, and not so many that it makes the news. At least not in Chicago, apparently. Since they've been around, everything's seemed even sadder and deader.
	The car hit the zombies and crumpled. Matt kept his foot on the gas, but the wheels just spun with sound and fury.
	Stephanie handed Matt a sawed-off shotgun and ammo. She held a sawed-off of her own. Matt's eyes were as wide as the rising moon.
	Whose is —
	Was my mom's. She left them in her will.
	She loaded the gun; was still topless. Her breasts were unfazed by the commotion.
	Ready? On three!
	Don't you want your shirt?
	There's no time! One, two, three!
	She pushed open the door and pulled the trigger. Pieces of Dora's head flew over the driveway and into the swamp. She reloaded and

shot at the drunk-shuffling zombie while Matt ducked and covered his head with his arms. She took Matt by the hand and led him into the swamp. Wayne and his date followed.

The road wasn't far, but they couldn't see it. The world was all shadows and roots and water and birds. The swamp grabbed at their feet, tried to take their shoes and whatever else it could get. They wanted the road, get to the road, the goal was the road. The road led out of the swamp, over the hill, away from the zombies, into the wide world of everywhere else. Get to the road; figure it out from there.

The zombies were somewhere behind them. They splashed through knee-deep water until they came to a fallen tree. They crawled over, propped their guns on the trunk and took aim. Matt thought about what McKean County would be like without Wayne. He would lose a loyal drinking buddy, a truth-teller, an unfettered alter ego. The large and lonely women at all the bars would lose a generous lover. Matt's eyes went misty as he realized Wayne was already gone. He shot Wayne in the head. Stephanie followed with a round through Wayne's date's perm.

They heard a noise; a splash from behind them. They turned and squinted into a lattice of dead branches and dead branch shadows. Twenty yards ahead, they saw an ambulance, bumper deep in the muck.

The driver's door was open and the seat was empty. They walked to the back. Matt could feel Stephanie shiver.

The back doors were open. The smell of iron and bile took the place of swamp rot. Two zombies were inside, eating a corpse. They each shot a zombie, and Stephanie shot the corpse for good measure. They turned away and ran.

The road was thirty, forty yards ahead. The road was the goal. Get to the road. A topless woman with large, wet breasts, holding a shotgun, running along the side of the road in a county redundant with men driving pick-up trucks? Somebody would stop and help them.

They were ten yards from the road when Stephanie lost her balance and sprawled forward. Her gun went off. Pellets sunk into her calf. Matt turned and watched two more zombies come around the ambulance.

Hurry! Get up! Get up!

My leg! I can't —

Matt yelled as he splashed back to her.

Come on! You have to get up! You have to get up now!

I can't move my leg!

The zombies, one male, one female, sloshed their way toward her feet. Though their faces were twisted and decayed, Matt recognized the Confederate flag ball cap.

Stephanie, don't look back!

She was crawling on her hands and knees, trying to find her gun in the muck. Matt couldn't help but notice that her tits didn't jiggle. So fake, he thought, so clearly fake.

Stephanie, keep moving, don't look back! Do not look back!

She stopped moving. She looked back.

Todd!

Not Todd! Not Todd! Stephanie! No!

She found a stump to help her stand. The female zombie was getting close. Matt took aim and removed her head. Stephanie screamed, Don't shoot Todd!

Matt took long leaps toward her and tried to reload in time.

Too late. Stephanie Taylor limped right into Zombie Todd Parnell's arms, and he tore a hole in her neck. Blood flowed through her cleavage like the Colorado through the Grand Canyon.

Matt shook his head at so many things, aimed at the stars and bars and pulled the trigger.

The Last Time Matt Lang Saw Stephanie Taylor

She was lying on her back in the swampy flood plain of the Allegheny River. She was mostly underwater; only the front-most half of her breasts, the half made possible by the implants, touched the night air. Two clouds parted, the moon shined through. It gave enough light for Matt to see the stretch marks on Stephanie's stomach. They looked like ripples below the water. Her bangs floated high above her eyes, waving goodbye. He looked at her eyes, at her mouth, which began to twitch. It tugged at his gut. He shot her mouth before she finished the smile. He reloaded, and shot her again.

Then he turned and walked toward the road.

This is a stand-alone excerpt from the novel *Fernweh*.

Stuck

MARK HOFFMAN and Susan Dixon, my parents, met in San Francisco during the Summer of Love, then moved into an aging farmhouse twenty miles outside of Guthrie, Oklahoma with the goal of bringing a piece of the hippie revolution back to my dad's hometown.

The farm belonged to my dad's grandfather, and his mom didn't want it, and his uncles didn't want it, and the neighbors all agreed that it wasn't worth the trouble to do anything but let the damn house and barn fall down and then take a match to the scraps. His mother was glad to let him have it, even if he did plan to live in sin and be the laughing stock of Logan County. She signed it all over to him, didn't want to keep any part of it because she didn't want the police knocking on her door when they found drugs and orgies and any other manner of devilry going on there. My dad hugged her tight and made her promise that she would come by for lunch after church on Sundays.

My parents worked hard, too hard to spend time on drugs and orgies, and I'd rather bleed out on this floor than consider otherwise. They had housemates come and go, most committed to the trappings of the revolution but not so much to the work and commitment and responsibility of the revolution. Shit won't grow on bad singing and even-worse poetry. They had one couple stay with them for four years before I was born, the Turners, originally from Atlanta. I remember them coming back to visit a few times. According to my parents, they didn't flake out or drop out or sell out, they just moved out. They missed the city, so they went to Oklahoma City to carry on the movement there.

If you know anything about Oklahoma politics, you know how successful my parents and their comrades were at bringing the revolution to where they lived. No sooner did they arrive than James Inhofe began his climb from the depths of hell to the United States Senate. I kept my permanent address in Oklahoma as long as I could because I considered it my patriotic and Christian duty to cast my vote against that monumental motherfucker. Him and Coburn. Christ almighty. Though every election seemed to bury them further and further under piles of nonsense, my parents loved Oklahoma. My dad still does, even with everything that happened, even though he's all alone down there.

My earliest memories are occupied with the faces of the visitors and transient workers who stayed with us. To a young boy, they were all fascinating and kind. My favorite was a Mexican migrant named Francisco. He lived with us from the spring to the fall of 1983. He showed me how to make slingshots and use them to kill mice. He spoke almost no English, but my mother spoke acceptable Spanish and he was happy to teach me any Spanish I wanted to learn *incluyendo los malditos, pero no dije tu mama. ¿Entiendes?* Francisco was on his way to Chicago where he hoped to find work in a factory or as a laborer, something that paid more and more often than seasonal farm work. He had an uncle there somewhere. I think about Francisco often, especially when I stand on the bridge at the Ashland stop and look at the city, rolled out from one end of the horizon to the other like wall-to-wall carpeting. I wonder if he is out there. I wonder if he is working, if he has a place to live. Did he even make it to Chicago? We never got a letter or anything after we dropped him at the Greyhound station in Tulsa.

The visitors stopped in 1984, the year my little brother, Conner, was born. My mom gave birth at home, in her bedroom, and Dad said he thought she was going to insist on delivering the child her own self. She pretty much ran the show right up until she became incoherent and handed the birth over to her two midwife friends. Though I had been close to the birth of several cows and goats, this was beyond me. I spent most of the birth playing outside under the bedroom window, just once peaking my head around the door jam.

"Honey," my mom said, buck naked, hair stuck to her face, gasping between contractions, "It's okay, you can come in if you want."

I did not. I fell asleep in the hall and woke to the sounds of crying, my mother's and new brother's. Before I could sit up on my own, my father lifted me in his arms and carried me into the room to meet Conner.

"Look, Jackson, this is your new baby brother. His name is Conner. You have to be nice to him and teach him how to be a good boy. What do you think?"

I thought he was all crying mouth and twitchy, unpredictable arms.

The fact that my brother was born at home did not win me any popularity points at school. In fact, it erased the few I'd earned by being able to build a slingshot, kill mice and curse in Spanish. Nobody but nobody knew what to make of me and my family. Their confusion was manifold:

> 1) My folks were not married — at least not officially sanctioned-before-God-and-these-witnesses married;
>
> 2) they were farmers, which was good, noble, respectable, but they were organic farmers, which was strange, irresponsible, reprehensible;
>
> 3) they were registered Democrats, but what did you expect when;
>
> 4) they just went ahead and invited Mexicans to come into their house and eat at their table.

And then giving birth at home, like animals or worse, like Indians. I was like a strange Moses, parting the seas of my fellow students as I walked down the hall, no one wanting to get too close to me.

Jackson's got his mom's pussy juice on him.

Jackson had his hands in his mom's snatch.
Jackson always has his hands in his mom's snatch.
Never mind that these same bastards, the base of the base of today's GOP:

1) pulled guts from deer on the regular (Tough, yes. Manly, yes. It also puts you close to deer snatch and deer ass and involves many juices),

2) came to school with cow shit on their boots (nothing wrong with cow shit, but wash your damn boots),

3) spit gobs of tobacco in drinking fountains and lockers and text books and lunches (this is indefensible) and,

4) in the locker room, after gym class, threw each others' clothes in the toilet right after taking a massive shit. Laughing and calling each other dipshits, they fished the clothes out, rinsed them off, and wore them the rest of the day (this is inexplicable).

By the time I was ten, I knew I had to leave and never look back.
I miss the sky, the tall grass, and the air in between. There were nights when, even though I was chattering my teeth loose, I couldn't bring myself to stop looking at the stars and go inside. The relentless wind, which drove some early pioneers insane, filled my head with white noise as it pushed the grass like a wave. I loved that it gets so goddamn hot in the summer and so goddamn cold in the winter. In the spring, nothing was better than sitting on my parent's front porch and watching a storm approach, seeing the sky get black then blacker, all shades of black, green-black, then smelling the rain before its arrival, knowing that as it moved east over the land people moved inside, powerless to do anything but sit and watch and wait.

There was a storm when my brother was just a year old. Huge storm, but it mostly missed town, cut a big swath through a wheat field, lots of tree branches torn down, power was out for two days. Everybody knew somebody who lost some cattle. Overall, though, the sense was we were blest, the prayers of the faithful availeth much, the storm missed us because God loved us more than others.

My parent didn't go to church. This was a big deal, further proof that we were beyond hope. My grandparents went to church, Prairie Presbyterian Church ("The Little Local Church with the Great Global Mission") and they took my brother and I there most Sundays. Presbyterians are generally a well-educated and reasonable breed of Christian — which made us threat level orange in the eyes of the Southern Baptists — but they were not reasonable enough for my dad. He was raised in that church, had nice memories of that church, but when it came time to be confirmed, to officially join the church in junior high, he declined. It just didn't make sense to him. He always needed things to make sense. One of the things that appealed to him about farming was that it made sense. If you did *this*, then you got *that*. If *that* didn't work, you changed the way you did *this*. If your plants were too large and the fruit was too small, there was too much nitrogen in the soil. If you didn't rotate your crops, the soil got depleted and nothing would grow well. If the chickens wouldn't go in to roost, then there was something wrong with their coop. The symbolism in the Bible drove my father crazy. Wasn't it enough to notice the goodness and beauty of the land? Why did it have to represent anything beyond itself? The Parable of the Sower — with the seeds that died and the seeds that thrived — is just sound farming advice. Consider the lilies of the field, see how they grow. Stop. That right there's your lesson.

My mom didn't go to church because in the year she turned fourteen and her sister, Stephanie, turned sixteen, her sister did proclaim, over a dinner of roast beef and mashed potatoes that she was in love with a girl in her class. There was much wailing and gnashing of teeth and then verily did her parents cast her sister into the outer darkness in the name of the Father, Son and Holy Spirit. The following Sunday, Father, Mother and Remaining Daughter stood in the front of their Four Square Gospel Church in Cheyenne, Wyoming and were hailed as conquering heroes, exemplars of Christian faith and conviction, because they showed neither grace nor mercy to a girl in love. After the service, many people remarked about the brave choice the Father and Mother had made, and what a fine example they set for Remaining Daughter. Yes, she was sad and angry now, but, in the fullness of time, she would see they did they right thing and she would thank them.

In the spring of that same year, Mr. Parker, her math teacher, asked my mom to stay after class to talk about her last test. She stayed in her seat in the front row while the rest of the class left, and Mr. Parker stood behind his desk. When they were alone in the room, he closed the door and moved to the front of the desk, leaning back against it as he spoke to my mom.

"Susan, you're not here to talk about your test. You're here because I have something for you."

My mom was confused and scared and silent. She sat still with her hands in her lap. Mr. Parker went back behind his desk and opened a drawer and removed an envelope. He came back around to the front of the desk and held the envelope out for my mom to take. She didn't move, she didn't know what it was. She looked at Mr. Parker and listened to the clock ticking on the wall in the back of the room.

"It's a letter from your sister. She sent it to my house. It came in a larger envelope with another letter to me. She wanted me to give this to you. She asked if she could send other letters to you like this. My inclination is to say yes, if that's what you want. Is that what you want, Susan?"

My mom took the letter and nodded her head yes. Mr. Parker leaned back against the desk once more.

"I had Stephanie in homeroom. I knew what was going on. What your parents did wasn't right. I won't tell them anything."

He looked back at the clock.

"The next class will be here soon. I'm so sorry, Susan. I hope getting the letter helps some."

My mom put the letter in her backpack and held in the tears. She nodded in Mr. Parker's directions as she left the room, but she was feeling to many feelings to be able to look him in the eye or tell him thank you.

I ask you, then, of these, the parents, the church, or the public school math teacher, who showed the greater kindness?

Mom got letters in this way for the rest of high school, letters from Boulder, Denver, Santa Fe, El Paso, Tucson, Los Angeles, San Francisco. The letters confirmed that Stephanie was alive, left a record of where she had been, and hinted at what she was doing — meeting, learning, singing, planting, creating, living. As vague as she was on the details of her activities, she was clear that she was doing them with the most amazing and beautiful people.

My mom studied hard, got a scholarship to the University of Wyoming, was told she couldn't go, turned eighteen, accepted the offer anyways, graduated, went to a party, never went back home. She slept on sympathetic couches until school started. Four years later she had a degree in nursing and a goal to find her sister.

They continued to write while my mom was in college. In the spring before she graduated, Mom got a letter from San Francisco. Stephanie said she planned to stay there for a while, maybe for life, and gave an address and invited Mom to join her. So after college, my mother followed the waves of hippies to Haight-Ashbury, even though she was scared to leave Wyoming, she didn't know what she was getting into, and she didn't make sure to wear flowers in her hair (For the umpteenth time, no! Your father was the real hippie, not me. Honest to God, I don't know why you think that is so funny. — My

Mom).

    She never had a chance of finding her sister. Haight-Asbury was overwhelmed with humanity — too many people, not enough places. Every plan that was in place — plans for housing, plans for food, plans for medical care — fell apart. My mother found the house where my aunt was supposed to be staying, but she wasn't there. Could they check again? They checked again. She wasn't there. Did they mind if she came in, to ask if anybody knew her? *No, that's cool; ask away.* Nobody knew her, but it was totally beautiful that she was trying to reconcile and reconnect. There was a church two blocks away; a lot of people without housing went there.

    "No, Stephanie wouldn't go into a church, not even here."

    "I can dig it; maybe try the park."

    It was in the park that she met my father, noticed not for the fact that he was naked (many other were, too), but because he was wearing a baseball mitt and playing catch and almost hit her in the head when he overthrew his partner. He was in San Francisco because things were so obviously broken, man, and when shit is broken, you have to fuckin' fix it. There's nothing magical or mystical about it.

    "We're just fixin' a flat tire. We're replacing the fuel injectors. We're the new fuel injectors."

    She explained that she was looking for her sister, explained why she hadn't seen her in so long. In deference to the gravity of the moment, my dad put on some pants. Together they moved through the park, looking for Stephanie, telling each other about their lives, and marveling at the spectacle. My dad offered to share his tent, an offer my mother accepted, having no other place to sleep. That night they gave each other a firm but polite handshake and then my father built a brick wall to separate the two of them as they slept and that's how they slept every night that summer.

    My mother never found her sister. She looked steady for three full weeks. She heard some wisdom: you've been a good sister, there's nothing else you can do. She heard some drivel: she belongs to the world now, she's out there she's in here she's everywhere. Everyone — even the drivel-spouter — was kind, concerned and willing to give her ample consolation drugs. She decided to stay for the summer. She and my dad lived in the tent in the park and spent almost all their time together. Some nights, after my dad fell asleep, Mom would walk to the church and sit in the sanctuary and, not pray, exactly, but hope really hard that Stephanie would walk in. She never did. Years later, I remember my mom getting a letter from New Mexico. The letter said Stephanie had died and been cremated. Her ashes were scattered in the desert.

Mom and Dad were in love by the end of the summer and by August and they began to make plans for the fall and beyond. The scene in Haight-Ashbury was played out. There were new and creative ways to live together, but there, in that place, with those people, was not it. My father told her about his grandma's farm, about how it was theirs if they wanted it. Did she want it? She wanted it. She would never go back to Wyoming, and had nothing in San Francisco. She only had Oklahoma, and the idea that she could be happy there. They never made plans to marry; they didn't see the point. My dad held the door of his pickup open and asked, "Susan will you do me the honor of getting in my truck and driving with me halfway across the goddamn country so we can change the world."

"I will."

Then: The country got angry, people got killed, we went to the moon, Nixon resigned, Nixon got pardoned, I got born, Reagan got elected, people got AIDS, Contras got aid, and people with televisions enjoyed M.A.S.H and the Huxtables. People without televisions missed Cliff and Clair and Punky Brewster and the Super Bowl Shuffle and Game Six. People without televisions remember going to their grandparents' house after school and sitting on their living room floor and watching the Challenger take off and explode and fall back down in pieces.

I watched the Challenger in my grandparents' living room with my family and my friend Steve, who was one of three friends I had growing up. Steve, Paul, Ernest. I spent the most time with Ernest, who lived in the next house over. He was two years younger than me, his mom cut his hair, which was pin-straight and the color of hay, and he often walked alone with his hands in his front pockets. I was his only friend. On many Saturdays, he would already be sitting on our porch when I woke up in the morning and came out to feed the animals.

"Hey, Jackson," he would say.

"Hey, Ernest."

"Are you feeding the animals?"

"Yes, Ernest. How did you guess?"

"Because you're wearing that blue shirt that you always wear to feed the animals and I always see you feed the animals when I come to sit on your porch."

"Do I always wear this shirt?"

"Sometimes you do. I bet the animals love you. Do you love them?"

"I don't think so Ernest. I think I just take care of them."

"Oh, I thought maybe you loved them."

I wish I could say I was nicer to Ernest in school, but I wasn't brave enough or sure enough to be kind to him in public. He was the buffer between me and the very bottom rung of the scholastic hierarchy. I was never actively cruel to him, but I was indifferent to the cruelty of others. When his books were knocked out of his hand, or when food was thrown at him at lunch, I would look the other way. Hey, Jackson, they would taunt, isn't that your best friend? Fuck off, I would reply. During each denial Ernest would look at me with eyes that said he understood what I was doing and he wasn't surprised, but still had hoped that this time would be different.

Ernest. His house was falling down. His mom was drunk. His

dad looked like he was ninety-eight, and an old, hard-lived ninety-eight. His oldest brother was in jail, his middle brother moved to Stillwater and didn't come back to visit much. Their yard, their porch, their kitchen, their living room was covered in goose shit. The whole property smelled like rotten eggs. The only well kept space was Ernest's room. His bed was always made, his clothes were always folded and put away, and his shoes were always lined up neatly along the wall.

"Someday I'm going to be a pilot and fly anywhere I want. What about you, what are you going to be?"

"Don't know, Ernest."

"Do you think a pilot would be cool? To be way up above everything?"

"That would be cool."

"Yeah, that's what I'm going to do."

Paul lived in Guthrie, right in Guthrie. He might as well have lived in Paris, so sophisticated and exotic did I find his circumstances. Paul's father traveled a lot, and, like a good, guilty father, filled his son's room with gifts collected from far and wide. His dad got him a jacket in Atlanta. He got him shoes in Dallas. He got him a sweatshirt in New York City. Paul had, get this, *been to New York City*. He said he was going to move there, no doubt. He had a map of the East Village on his wall.

"The Village still has cool shit if you know where to look, but it's so fucking gentrified, you know?"

I did not. I was eleven. So was he.

Paul also had cable, which meant he had MTV, which meant I would spend the night whenever I could and we would stay up late and watch *Yo! MTV Raps*. In the wee hours, De La Soul and Tribe Called Quest crept across Paul's yard, opened his bedroom window and climbed on in. They showed us postcards and told us stories. "Bonita Applebum" was the outward sign of an inward truth that I had known but never before seen: Logan County was not enough.

Steve and I played Little League together, me at shortstop, he at second. For reasons that defied geography we both cheered for the New York Mets. I because I saw Q-Tip wear a Mets hat while giving a tour of his old neighborhood for an MTV special on gun violence, Steve because the Mets won the first and only major league game he had ever been to, against the Cardinals, in the old Busch Stadium. Though planted far from the five boroughs, the roots of our affection were deep enough to sustain us through Pendelton's homerun in '87, and Scioscia's homerun in '88, Strawberry's departure in '90, and then those sad, lost years when Bernard Gilkey was our best player and the oh so close pain of '99 and 2000 and then 2006 and 20 — Christ. Fucking Mets.

Steve lived on the edge of Logan County where the cows could have taken over in ten minutes if they had any gumption; such was their numerical superiority. Tornados could lie down and roll along the ground and not come within miles of anything built by hands. His dad still thought they lived too close to town.

Such isolation fosters insular thinking and paranoia, zen-like attention to one's immediate surroundings, uncontrollable weeping, drug use and cutting, or creativity. Steve's dad was paranoid; Steve and I tried to be creative. Our attempts at creativity did not always pan out.

One summer afternoon, around three-o'clock in the afternoon, Steve and I thought, Hey, let's shut Pete in the foldout coach. Pete was Steve's cousin. Pete was game. With the couch in bed mode, he laid across the width of it. We made the first fold.

"Can you breath, Pete?"

"Yes."

We pushed the couch into couch mode.

"Can you breath, Pete?"

"Yes."

We replaced the cushions.

"How you doin', Pete?"

"Good."

We sat on the cushions, just for a while, just long enough to make it official. High five! We removed the cushions. We gave the couch a pull. The couch didn't move. We pulled again. It didn't move.

A muffled voice: "Guys, I'm ready to get out now."

"We're working on it, Pete."

Again, we pulled. Nothing. That couch was stuck, and we were pretty sure that Pete being folded inside had something to do with it.

"Guys, it's getting hard to breath in here."

"Pete, don't panic, but the couch is stuck."

Pete panicked. "Stop fucking around! Let me out!"

"We're not fucking around! The couch is stuck!"

"That's not funny, assholes! Let me out of the fucking couch!"

"Pete, I swear to God we are not joking. You are stuck in the couch."

Steve called his dad at work and explained what we had done. He understood.

"You gotta be fucking shittin' me! That's the goddamn dumbest thing I've ever heard!"

His dad was Paul Bunyan, a monster whose singular presence may have been enough to keep the cows of Logan County in check. He didn't drive from work; he strode across town with lumberjack steps. He stomped in the room and freed Pete with a mighty tug. Our creativity was lost on him.

"Jesus Christ, I'm going back to work. Next time you'll stay stuck in the goddamn couch. Dipshits."

Skipping Stones

SHE DECIDED she wanted to learn to skip stones.

Early one morning, while her parents still slept, she left her house on Boundary Street and headed down into Panther Hollow. Collecting stones along the way, she made her way to the lake. She took her place some distance from an old, Italian man sitting on the red, white and green picnic table near the edge of the water. She weighed the first stone in her hand, practiced the angle, and then released it. It sank with an audible plop. So did the next one. So did the next one. All the stones sank that first day. She wiped her palms on the front of her jeans and walked away.

She was back the next week with more stones. The same man was there, at the same spot at the same table. He watched as she threw stone after stone after stone into the water. Plop. Plop. Plop. Notes of failure. After her hands were empty, she looked at the spots where the stones had gone under, wiped her palms again, and left.

Another week. Same time. Same girl. Same man. Same table. Different stones. More plops. He could tell she was throwing the stones too hard and at the wrong angle. Too much shoulder, not enough wrist. She was working too hard. She needed to find the right angle, flick her wrist just so, and trust that the stone would do the work that it needed to do. The stone didn't want to sink any more than she wanted it to sink. Given half a chance, the stone would stay above water until it decided it had enough and would slide into the water contented. He was just about to stand to tell her when she figured it out. Skip. Skip skip. Skip skip skip skip. She found the right angle, the right rhythm. Her arm was swinging loose, and she was flicking her wrist at just the right time, and the stones were dancing across the lake, as happy as stones could possibly be.

The last stone just brushed the water and skipped seventeen times before it stopped farther away from shore than the girl thought possible. It made a small ripple as it went under and the man thought, *That's the best we can hope for, isn't it?* And he was happy with this thought. And the girl was happy with how she skipped that last stone, so she wiped her palms on her jeans and went home.

"Back to Ur" was first published in *Pulp Metal Magazine* in the Summer of 2015.

Back To Ur

Once upon a time, when there were only a few folks living on Earth, and the Lord God could take the time to address them individually, God spoke to Abraham.

"Abraham", said God, while Abraham was grilling lamb kebobs in his back yard. Abraham flinched when he heard his name coming from an unspecified place above and behind his left shoulder.

*

Abraham knew it was God, because God was always talking to him, and the voice always came from the same place. The first time he heard it, he was living in Ur of the Chaldees and still going by his given name, Abram. The voice told him to leave his home in Ur, even though his friends, family, hometown sports teams, and the diner where they always saved him the best seat up by the window were there; and wander in the desert, even though the desert was dry and dangerous, and God was vague about where exactly he should go. The second time he heard it, the voice told him that he was no longer going to be called Abram, but Abraham, even though Abram was the name on his birth certificate, marriage certificate, bank accounts, and credit reports. The third time he heard it, the voice told him to cut off his foreskin, even though it wasn't causing him or anybody else any trouble whatsoever.

Abraham always did what God asked, unlike most people who, when asked to leave home or remove a body part, either ignored God or chose a lesser sacrifice, like setting up a swear jar and putting a quarter in it each time they cursed. Abraham, though, feared God, and feared what would happen if he failed the tests, even as he hoped each test would be the last, hoped that moving away from home, and changing his name, and cutting off the end of his dick would be enough for God. But it never was. God couldn't get over the fact that Abraham kept doing whatever God asked, so God kept coming up with more tests, curious as to what Abraham's limit might be.

*

"Abraham," God said.

Abraham flinched, but knew it was no use trying to hide or pretend he didn't hear. "Here I am", he replied.

God continued, "Take your son, your only son, Isaac, whom you love, and go to the land of Moriah, and offer him there as a burnt offering on one of the mountains that I shall show you."

God didn't really want Abraham to burn his son, God only wanted to get a rise out of him, to see the look on his face when he finally reached his breaking point. Through all the tests God had given him, God had never heard Abraham curse, or even raise his voice. God loved it when people lost it, delighted in seeing people at their wit's end. God put people to the test, not to see *if* they'd fail, but *how*. How much cursing, how much kicking, how much punching at the air with mortal futility? Abraham, though, was a tough cookie. He always did what God asked without complaint, so God came up with the most absurd test yet, sure that it would at last trigger the spectacle of Abraham throwing down his tongs and yelling, "Leave me alone you fucking motherfucking fuck!" Maybe, if God was lucky, Abraham would kick a rock and hurt his toe and unleash a second wave of profanity.

But Abraham slowly took the kebobs off the grill and put the fire out. He didn't say anything, he swallowed his feelings, felt a little twinge in his mind, and obeyed God like he always did, with the silent hope that this test would be the last, and from this point on God would leave him alone.

*

The next morning, Abraham woke up early and loaded up his truck. Then he went and knelt beside Isaac, shook his shoulder, and said, "Wake up, son, it's time to go."

Isaac sat up and saw his father standing by his bed, two servants standing behind him. "Where are we going?" he asked.

"We are going to travel for a distance, and then make an offering that will please the Lord."

*

As they drove, Isaac couldn't help but notice that there was not a sheep, nor ram, nor fatted calf tied in the back of the truck like there usually was. Isaac was young, but he had helped with offerings before. He knew what was missing. He looked in the rearview and saw the two servants crouched in the bed and wondered which of those poor souls would have to die to satisfy God.

God, too, wondered about Abraham's plan.

*

After they had been driving for three days, they stopped. Abraham looked at a hill in the distance and mulled over what he would tell his wife, Sarah. "The Lord giveth and the Lord taketh away?" That sounded trite. "His ways are not our ways, dear Sarah?" Not quite. "Ours is not to question why, ours is just to do and die?" Maybe something like that. Abraham put the truck in park and rapped the back window with his knuckles, the signal to the servants that they'd arrived.

"Stay here with the truck," he said to them, "the boy and I will go over there; we will worship, and then we will come back to you."

Isaac was confused. If they were going to make a sacrifice to the Lord God, they were lacking a key ingredient, namely, the animal to be sacrificed. Isaac wondered if Abraham was starting to lose it, thought maybe his mind was slipping. Even as they walked away from the truck, it seemed as if the old man was arguing with himself. And were those tears rolling down his cheeks?

Isaac asked, "Father?"

Abraham stopped, wiped his face, and said, "Here I am, my son."

Isaac went on, "The fire and the wood are here, but where is the lamb for a burnt offering?"

God had seen enough. God hadn't got the hoped for reaction, and God was getting a little concerned. There was no part of God that believed Abraham was actually going to go through with it, but God worried about Isaac and the mental toll this was taking on him.

"Abraham," God said.

Abraham heard the voice, and flinched, as he always did, but this time he was looking down at Isaac, and was lost in the boy's eyes. He saw in them a multitude of generations, and then he saw the boy, just the boy, looking back at him with fear, doubt, hope and trust, but a trust that was slipping away, a trust that was only there because, out in the desert, far from home, what choice did a boy have but to trust his father? The twinge in Abraham's mind turned to a snap, followed by a long, slow unraveling.

"You'll see, son," Abraham said, and he and Isaac walked on together.

*

They came to the top of hill and Abraham built an altar, laid the wood, and grabbed his son and bound him fast. God shouted to get his attention, but Abraham was too far-gone, he had the wide-open eyes of a madman, the eyes of Cain before he crushed the head of Abel. God shouted again. Abraham raised up the knife. God shouted a third time, but nothing.

God needed a new plan.

*

Violence was a design flaw that God had long been ashamed of. Cain was the first, and God had hoped he was the last, a one-time glitch. But since that day, God had seen brothers kill brothers, strangers kill strangers, husbands kill wives, and cities attack cities. Some of it was planned, some of it was random, all of it tore at God's very being. God hated it, but could do nothing about it, because people had choices. Maybe this was another design flaw.

Abraham, of course, always chose to do what God asked. God's new plan was to put this obedience to better use, but first God needed to get his attention.

Normally, not a problem, but Abraham wasn't responding to God's voice this time. This time God had to send an angel, and the angel called out "Abraham, Abraham."

Abraham stood, knife at the boy's throat, and shook his head to try to clear the daze.

"Here I am."

"Do not lay a hand on the boy or do anything to him! Behold, I present another sacrifice!"

Abraham cocked his head, uncertain as to what that angel was holding. The angel explained:

"It is called an Ar-15. It is an assault rifle, and it has but one purpose, which is to kill people. It is a symbol of all the violence that has been and ever will be. Remove the boy, and place this on the altar instead! Sacrifice this, so the world may live in peace!"

Abraham stared at the weapon, his eyes still wide. It looked to him like some kind of mechanical reptile. He thought about what it would feel like to hold something so deadly. He imagined the sound it would make, the vibrations that would run through his body, down to the very earth. If he had that gun, he wouldn't fear God or anyone else ever again. If God tried to put him to another test, he'd shoot the sky until God moved on down the road. He'd change his name back to Abram, go back to Ur, and take his rightful seat in his favorite diner, and if anyone was sitting there, why, he'd shoot them, too.

So Abraham did take the knife and cut his son's throat clear down to the spine, while the angel watched and screamed. Isaac's blood did run down and pool on the ground. Abraham lit the fire and the boy burned. Abraham took the gun from the angel and slung it over his shoulder. He set off toward Ur, as the smoke from the altar filled the sky.

Manila, Mindoro, Manila

Manila

THE AIR outside Ninoy Aquino International Airport smelled like diesel, chicken, fruit, and labor. Matt Lang held a bag in each hand as he looked for Andrea in the crowd of people waiting to greet the new arrivals. Andrea was a head taller than the rest of the crowd and the only one with long, blond hair pulled back into a ponytail. Her arms were folded across her chest; her head was tilted to one side. Matt thought she looked tired.

When Andrea saw him she straightened her head, took a deep breath in, and waved her hand over her head as if she needed to make herself more noticeable. The people around her cleared the way for her to greet Matt Lang with a hug. A few people clapped. An older woman, who neither of them knew, took their picture.

*

Andrea was staying in a small apartment off a courtyard behind a church. The apartment had a kitchen/dining room, a bedroom, and a bathroom. The kitchen/dining room had a sink, a water cooler, a hotplate, a plug-in teakettle, a table, and two chairs. The bedroom had a mattress and piles of books on the floor. The bathroom had a toilet with no seat and a large garbage bin filled with water. The bin of water had a bucket floating in it. Overhead fluorescent lights lit each room.

So this is it, Andrea said.

Matt saw a mouse run behind the sink. He kept the news to himself. He said it was nice and tried to believe his own words.

You're freaked out.

I'm not freaked out, I'm fucking exhausted.

You can put your things in the bedroom. Are you hungry? Thirsty?

So thirsty.

Matt put his things in the bedroom and took a seat at the table. The room was not air-conditioned and he was well on his way to sweating through every inch of his t-shirt. Andrea filled a plastic cup with water from the water cooler.
 Is it safe?
 The water?
 Yeah, is it safe to drink?
 It's from the cooler. It's delivered.
 Yeah, but —
 It's safe.
 Matt Lang had never left the United States before. In fact, he had never been further west than Iowa or further south than Kentucky. By his own estimation, he spent eighty-five percent of his time in Pennsylvania. He was born there, went to school there, and now he lived and taught high school history there, in Erie. When Andrea asked him to come visit, he had to ask her how one goes about getting a passport.
 He drank the water in one take. His shirt felt like moss, attached to his skin permanently. He felt like a creature not made for this new world, like he had gills on his back that were fighting for oxygen in a hostile atmosphere. He drank two more cups. He wanted to touch her, to kiss her, but his sweatiness disturbed him and he assumed it would have the same effect on her.
 I feel disgusting. I need a shower.
 Um, I don't really have a shower so much.
 He looked to the water-filled garbage bin with the bucket floating therein. Andrea confirmed his suspicions.
 You scoop the water and pour it on your head.
 Minutes later, as he stood naked before the bucket, he couldn't help but feel that, for the first time since he was four, he was going to fail at taking a bath. He dipped the bucket into the water, raised it over his head, and dumped it.

There was a frozen moment between when the water first hit and when he released a scream unworthy of a full-grown man. He was certain he had died and his soul had been ripped from his chest. How could this water be so cold, given that it was sitting in a room so hot? What kind of sinister physics was at play? The water shattered any former frame of reference and washed it down the drain.

Andrea poked her head in the bathroom.

Are you okay?

He needed time to form his words. His testicles were somewhere just below his lungs.

It's so cold.

I forgot to tell you.

Jesus Christ.

You'll get used to it.

What the hell was wrong with her? You'll get used to stabbing yourself in the heart with an icicle? Maybe she was fucking with him. This was some Southeast Asian hazing ritual. He would step out of the bathroom to a room full of people laughing at him because he fell for it. Then he would be taken to the real shower, a proper shower, a shower that had some way to regulate the temperature.

While he was drying off, minutes after almost dying from arctic shock, he felt the heat crawl back in, first through the back of his neck and soon through his whole body and then back out in the form of still more sweat. He was dry for, at most, one full second. He didn't put on a shirt. He sat at the table and tried not to move, tried to not even take deep breaths.

If you're still too hot, there's AC in the bedroom.

That sounds amazing.

Just pull the door shut.

He turned on the window unit and lay down on the mattress. He fell asleep with the light on.

*

Matt Lang woke up at two-thirty in the morning, which was two-thirty in afternoon in Erie. If he were there, he would be outside in the summer sun; here, he was inside in the dark. The AC was jet powered; it could not have been over sixty degrees in the room. In this strange land, was there no happy medium between freezing and stifling? Andrea was sound asleep next to him, still dressed in the t-shirt and slacks she had been wearing earlier. He rummaged through his clothes until he found the one long-sleeved shirt he brought. He went to have a look outside.

He stood in the doorway and stared at an empty courtyard. The ground was dirt, and a lone tree grew in the far corner. An iron gate provided a break in the concrete rectangle that closed in the yard. Through the gate, Matt Lang could see the street, empty, quiet, illuminated by a street lamp on the corner. He watched a woman waddle into view. She stopped in front of the gate and wrapped her hands around the bars. She leaned her head against the gate, her wispy hair visible in the lamp light. Matt Lang saw a dog limping behind her. One of its back legs was broken and sticking to the side at an angle that made Matt a little nauseous. He was getting hot again, so he went back inside and went back to bed.

*

Four hours later he woke up and heard Andrea in the kitchen, talking with another woman, older and Filipina by the sound of her voice. Through his sleepiness, he caught pieces of conversation: activist, motorcycle, two children, again, daylight, reality. He propped himself on his elbows and heard the older woman say, clearly, before she left, Everyday we wonder who will be next.

Matt Lang stepped into the kitchen, on the way to the bathroom.

Andrea was standing by the burner, frying what looked like sardines.

As he pissed he wondered who the older woman was and what she was talking about, what *who will be next* meant, and if there was going to be anything else for breakfast, and if there wasn't, was he going to be able to stomach the sardines? His stream looked like concentrated orange juice, but it smelled just like piss. He wondered about washing his hands. What were the rules? Could he use the bucket water for this? What other water was there? Seeing none, he used the bucket water. He dipped his hands in and pulled them right back out, certain that that was some breach of etiquette at best, that he had contaminated the entire water supply at worst. How could hand washing not be self-evident?

Back in the kitchen, Matt took a seat and asked about the woman, and the conversation. Andrea answered while piling rice on two plates, and placing sardines on the rice.

Her name is *Ate* Dora. Spelled A-t-e, but pronounced like that: *Ah-tay*. It's an honorific, it means older sister. She's been my primary support here, helped me make all my connections, set me up with all the women I've interviewed. She's been at it a long time. We were talking about the latest killing. There was a strike at a Coca-Cola plant south of here and they sent in goons to break it up. That night the lead organizer disappeared. Two days later they found his body half-buried in a rice field ten kilometers away. He'd been shot in the back of the head and his tongue was cut out and stuffed in his shirt pocket.

Matt looked at his breakfast. Latest killing implied there had been prior killings, probably a string of killings. Andrea never mentioned any of this in her emails or over Skype. Matt cut a piece of the fish with the side of his spoon and scooped it up with an ample amount of rice. The whole bite tasted like oil and salt, even with all that rice.

I had no idea.

Most people don't. That's why I'm writing the book.

I thought your book was about sex workers.

It is, but sex work or working for Coke, different windows into the same world.

Matt and Andrea ate the rest of their breakfast. Matt needed several drinks of water to get through all that salty fish.

*

They left Andrea's apartment at a little after five-thirty that evening, Matt having gone back to bed after breakfast, fallen asleep, and dreamt about a leaky pipe that couldn't be fixed, raw sewage dripping onto his arms and face as he worked. Though the sun was lower in the sky, the temperature had not dropped, the city was hanging onto all of the heat of the day — from the sun, from the cars, from the people — and was unwilling or unable to let any of it go. The heat was taking up space.

How long is the walk?

Not even half a mile.

I might die.

It will be cooler by the bay.

This was false. When they got to the bay, it was no different. There was not a breeze to be felt. The water was as still and flat as a putting green.

I'm assuming people don't swim here.

People shouldn't swim here. I'm not even sure it's safe to look at directly. But people do. Swim, I mean. And fish.

I can't believe anything can even live in there.

Maybe nothing can. Maybe people just do it because that's what you do when you're next to water. Most people in most times and in most places, when they live next to water, they grab a pole, or net, head down to the shore and fish. For 99.99% of human history that would be appropriate behavior, maybe people who fish the bay just want to feel normal.

They sat side by side on a knee wall as they watched the sun drop and turn red. Andrea leaned her head on Matt Lang's shoulder. He liked it in spite of the humidity. A small boy ran up to him, lightly touched him on the arm and then ran away as his friends laughed from behind a small tree. A vender wheeled a cart down the sidewalk. The vender was silent, his wares a mystery. Maybe he was on his way home, maybe he was exhausted. Another couple took a seat on the wall a few yards away. For no good reason, Matt Lang thought they were German. The man said something and the woman gave a loud and deep laugh. Matt Lang and Andrea got up to leave but a woman blocked their way. She had spider web thin hair, only a few teeth, and on her cheek was a mole so large it nearly pinched her eye shut. She hiked up her dress to show legs covered with days of Manila soot, and took an ample, pungent piss.

*

At the table at a restaurant at the end of a pier, Matt Lang could catch the slightest hint of a breeze. He leaned back and tried to absorb as much as he could. He sat with his back to the bay, looking back at the city. Roxas Boulevard stretched to his right. Lined with palm trees and hotels, lit with neon lights, from his seat it looked Miami-elegant. It helped that he'd had three beers.

It's so weird you live here.

Well, I've only been here for a few months. I don't really *live* here.

No, you live here. I mean, you knew how to get me from the airport, you know how to go out and get lunch, you have friends stop by for breakfast, you have favorite restaurants. You live here.

I know a few places in a giant city. If I leave this little neighborhood, I'm fucked, helpless as a little child.

The waiter came and patiently stood by their table, pen held to pad, ready to take their order. He did not speak until Andrea looked up to order. After the waiter left, Matt Lang asked Andrea how long she thought he would have stood there.

Hard to say.

So polite.

Polite to a fault.

A fault?

I mean, they fall all over themselves to make sure tourists are happy, meanwhile, their own lives are a mess and the country is falling apart.

That's not that bad, though, right? I mean, it's nice to be nice.

But it's fucking pathological here. It's beyond being nice and polite, it's a real inferiority complex. It's like they think they deserve to be shit on. I heard one guy say, with all seriousness, that what Filipinos eat for dinner, we in America feed to our dogs. He really, in his heart, believed this.

Matt Lang had a hard time focusing on the conversation. At another restaurant, at an adjacent pier, a band was playing "The Flame" by Cheap Trick. The lead singer's take on Robin Zander was betrayed by only the slightest trace of an accent.

Is the food here bad or something?

No, it's fine. Most of it is delicious. Wait until you taste this tuna that's coming. Out of the fucking world. But most people here just can't believe that they have anything worthwhile.

What about your friend? Dora, was it?

Yeah, Dora. She's different. She's in the minority. She's a hardcore activist. She's been at it since Marcos was in power. No, she doesn't think she's inferior. Maybe closer to the opposite. Most of the time I think she just wants me to go home. Yankee go home. The rest of the time, she's glad I'm here listening to the stories.

The waiter brought their food, the lead singer nailed the key change, and Matt Lang took a bite of tuna. It was the best fish he'd ever tasted.

Mindoro

In the morning they went to Mindoro to spend two days on the beach. On the ferry they were two tourists among many, including a middle-aged white man and his Filipina companion. Matt couldn't say for sure, but she looked at least twenty years younger than him. The rest of the passengers were smiling, pointing, taking pictures, watching dolphins jump next to the ferry, but the woman sat with her hands in her lap and her eyes fixed on her hands. The man sat pressed against her, one hand wrapped around her shoulder, the other hand pulling at her chin. He spoke with an Australian accent.

Come on. Give me a smile. Come on. One smile? We're at beach. Smile for me.

She tilted her chin towards him, closed her eyes and surrendered a sketch of a smile.

That's better.

*

It was already dark when the boat docked. Andrea got down and got away as fast as she could, leaving Matt to collect their bags and give out tips. He was already on the beach when the Aussie took a place next to him, right at the end of the boat ramp. The Aussie held out a hand to each person as they stepped off — *There ya go now, watch your step now* — and then offered to help an older couple carry their luggage to their hut. Matt could hear the Australian asking the couple where they were from as he and they and his companion walked away from the boat, down the row of huts, in the direction of the restaurant at the center of the resort. It was long past time for dinner, and Matt wondered, as he gathered the bags, tipped the luggage attendant and declined an offer to be escorted by flashlight, if Andrea would join him for a quick bite, or if she was in for the night.

She was in for the night. She said she was tired and wanted to rest, wasn't feeling hungry anyways. Matt said he needed something to eat and she told him fine, go ahead, eat if he really needed to eat. He felt chastised by her tone, guilty for having an appetite, but he was, in fact, hungry, and there was only one place to get food. He promised to be quick.

In the restaurant, he saw the Australian and his companion at the bar. The Australian motioned for him to come over. He hesitated for a second before accepting the invitation, reasoning that he was lonely, he'd never met an Australian before, and maybe it wasn't what it looked like after all.

The Aussie extended his hand as Matt took the stool next to him.

Hey mate, flyin' solo tonight, are ya?

Matt accepted the hand, which was softer than he expected an Aussie's hand to be. Less rugged outback, more comfortable corner office.

Yeah, she's in bed already.

You the night owl?

I'm the jet-lagged owl.

Jet-lagged owl needs a beer, then.

The Aussie bought three beers, even though the woman he was with had finished less than a third of her first. Matt played detective, looking him over, with quick glances, for reasons to like him, reasons to hate him. He didn't have a wedding ring, he wore a light blue t-shirt over broad shoulders and a developing beer belly, tan shorts, and flip-flops. His blond hair was cut short, parted to one side. His fingernails looked as if they'd been manicured, and he had a watch that looked like maybe it was priced in the thousands, so he was making money in that imagined corner office. Matt guessed he was between forty-two and forty-six-years-old. He saw no reason not to like him, expect for the fact that he was with a Filipina who looked a year or two shy of eighteen, who was probably not sitting there for free.

The Aussie picked up his beer and tilted it towards Matt.

Cheers, mate.

Matt reciprocated. The two bottles clinked.

Cheers. Thanks.

Name's Brian. This here's Maria.

He leaned back and pointed a thumb at the woman, who was hunched over, looking at — no, looking into — her cell phone. Matt reached across to shake her hand. She took his hand with the ends of her fingers and gave a slight shake and nod, without looking his way.

Matt said, Nice to meet you.

She replied with another nod and released his hand. Brian put his arm around her.

She's quiet at first, but once she warms up, she can be a feisty one.

The way he said *feisty*, kind of growled it out, like he was talking to a puppy, made the back Matt's neck stiffen just a bit, his jaw tighten just a touch, and a small knot form in his stomach. In an open-air restaurant, on a wide, flat beach, next to a deep and endless sea, Matt felt trapped. He couldn't imagine how the girl felt. Brian was pulling at her chin again, and again asking her to give a smile.

Well, if not for me, how 'bout for our new friend here? Will ya do it for — Sorry, mate, I didn't get your name.

Matt finished his beer and placed the empty bottle in front of Brian. It's Matt.

Brian pulled Maria's chin more firmly and kissed her on the mouth. The bartender took the empty bottle and quickly wiped the table, careful not to make eye contact or seem obtrusive or even present in any way. Brian released Maria and turned his attention back to Matt.

First time in the Philippines, Matt?

Matt didn't want to admit how provincial he was, saw it as a kind of weakness, but he was too provincial to even begin to be able to fake having been to the Philippines, or anywhere, before.

Yeah. First time out of the country.

Wow. Cheers then. Welcome to paradise. Lemme get you another beer.

Before Matt could say yes or no, Brian was signaling for more beers, one for Matt, one for him, one for Maria. Maria hadn't taken a drink since Matt arrived; the beers she had were getting warmer and flatter by the second. Nonetheless, Brian said, Drink up, love. Shame to waste perfectly good beers.

Matt remembered being nineteen, home from college for the summer, at a party with friends from high school. After the party, he rode home with those friends and a girl they'd all met there, a young girl, fifteen, maybe sixteen. Matt was riding shotgun, Mike was driving, and the girl was in the back with Derrick and Tony. She was passed out drunk and his friends took turns fucking her, even stopped the car so Mike could take a turn. They asked Matt if he wanted a turn. All the way to Matt's house. None of them knew the girl's name. Matt said no, but did nothing to stop them. They dropped Matt off, and presumably kept going until they got tired. Matt didn't go back home for summer after that.

As Brian kissed and whispered to Maria, Matt reached for a cell phone he didn't have, a nervous tick, a wish for a graceful way out of the situation. There was no television to look at, not even many other people: the bartender on the other end of the bar, two blonde women over by a window, and Maria and Brian.

Brian asked, Where in the States are you from? I'm assuming the States, right?

Matt wiped his hands on his thighs as he answered.

Yeah, the States. Pennsylvania. Erie is the city.

Erie? That's the name? Sounds bleak, mate.

It is.

Well, this is the place for you then. Like I said, paradise.

Matt noticed how tan Brian was, and how white he was, how relaxed Brian seemed, compared to how tense he felt, how at home

Brian acted, verses how out of place he was.

You seem like you've been here before.

As if to prove the point, Brian took out his phone, to check a text message he just got.

Yeah, I'm here for business quite a bit. Mostly in Manila. This trip wrapped up quicker than planned, so I have a few extra days. How 'bout you, what brings you here?

My girlfriend is doing research for a book she's writing on the sex industry.

Matt surprised himself with the directness of his answer, but it was also a relief, a sudden change of pressure, a river reversing its flow. Though he couldn't know for sure, it looked to Matt like the back of Brian's neck stiffened just a bit, his jaw tightened just a touch, and a small knot formed in his stomach. Brian dug his thumbnail into the label etched in the beer bottle. Seeing the shift in Brian's demeanor made him feel strong and bold. He imagined telling Andrea about his night, he imagined her proud of him. Maria was hunched even more, curled inward, trying to crawl inside herself.

Brian said, I guess that's quite a problem, isn't?

I guess so. You've been around. Have you seen any of it?

If he had been at a bar back in Erie, he wouldn't have been so brave, but on the beach, in the Philippines, he felt a courageous mix of an outsider's freedom with insider's knowledge. He didn't have to defer and deflect like the locals; he could play by different rules, be direct, assertive, look at Brian, and Maria, and the Coca-Cola signs around the restaurant and see the larger system of oppression that he would help disrupt by continuing to ask just the right questions.

I mean, from what I hear from my girlfriend, it's foreign business that drives a big part of it.

Brian squeezed his bottle tighter and dug his nail in deeper.

You'll have to ask your girlfriend about that, mate.

Matt had never been in a fight in his life, and he didn't necessarily want his first to be with a large Australian, even one with soft, manicured hands, but something about the jet-lag, and the feisty, and the two beers, and the salty air, had him feeling aggressive. He looked around Brian, to Maria.

How did you two meet?

Brian squared his shoulders to Matt, blocking Maria from his sight.

Are you gonna buy the next round, mate? Or are we done here?

Matt stood up, and saw the bartender over Brian's left shoulder, wiping and re-wiping the same spot on the bar, looking like he wanted them all to go to bed.

I think we're done. Thanks for the beers.

He looked around Brian to speak to Maria.

It was nice to meet you.

She hadn't moved much.

*

When Matt woke up the next morning, he was alone in the bed. He found Andrea sitting in a chair on the porch, reading.

Good morning.

Good morning, she said, looking up at him, her eyes squinting against the brightness. Then she went back to her book.

I'm going to get some breakfast. Do you want to come with me?

She shook her head while reading.

Matt put his hand on her shoulder. She didn't react one way or another.

If this is about that guy? Look I ran into him last night and —

It's not about that guy. It's about me wanting to relax. No matter who's there, that place won't be relaxing. This is relaxing. That place — she wiped at the air with her palm — Not relaxing. But you can go,

Then she looked up at him and squinted into the sun.

*

Matt left her on the porch and walked back toward the restaurant, worried that he'd failed some sort of test. Yes, Brian would be there, maybe, but there would also be tables and coffee, and he could sit at a table, and drink a coffee, and look at the ocean. He'd never sat at a table, and drank a coffee, and looked at the ocean.

Brian wasn't in the restaurant when Matt got there. Matt found a seat at a table with a view of the ocean and ordered a plate of papaya and a cup of coffee. He was trying to enjoy the quiet warmth of the morning, not think about Brian and the word feisty, not think about Andrea and how much she seemed like a stranger, when he heard an Australian-sized laugh rumble down the beach.

Brian was walking among a group of children; a jolly, blonde giant teaching the basics of Australian rules football, using a ball he must have brought from home, a half-dozen black-haired boys looking up at him as he spoke, and chasing after him when he showed them how to run with the ball, bounce it, handball it, and kick it. He (or someone) had tied a rope between a palm tree and the post of a gazebo. He used this as the goalposts. He lined the boys up and had them practice kicking the ball through the goalposts. Maria was nowhere to be seen.

Brilliant, that's brilliant! Now, you know what signal the official makes when the kick is good? He does this.

Brian stood stiff-backed, head high, and snapped his arms into place at his sides, ninety degrees at each elbow, index and middle fingers pointed forward. The children fell all over themselves with laughter.

Again!

You want me to do it again? You have to score a goal!

So they kicked goals, and Brian signaled, and they laughed, and they kicked goals, and Brian signaled, and they laughed, and then Brian kicked goals, and they took turns signaling, and Brian laughed and they all laughed together.

Brian saw Matt watching and gave him a salute, or the tip of an imaginary hat, and declared, It's brilliant morning, isn't it, mate?

Matt asked, Where's Maria?

If Brian heard, he didn't acknowledge. He kicked the ball through the goal and he and the boys chased after it.

*

Andrea's notes and her laptop sat untouched on the table next to the bed. None of his business, Matt supposed, but wasn't she going to work on her book? Wasn't that part of the reason they came to the beach? He wondered about the point. She wasn't working, she wasn't talking to him, she spent much of their time at the beach standing at the edge of the water. Matt would join her sometimes, and they would talk about neutral things, like the undeniable beauty of the place. He'd take her hand and squeeze it, and she'd wait a moment and then squeeze it back.

*

On another afternoon on which Andrea wanted to be alone, Matt Lang sat in the restaurant by a window and filled in postcards to send to his mother, who wanted pictures of the beaches, and his friend Dave, who was certain that Matt Lang was going to get violently ill, kidnapped, or both. As he wrote, he saw a brittle-boned hand reach through the window. He followed the hand up a worn out arm to find the face of an old woman with thin hair, sparse teeth, and a large mole that was impossible to forget. With her other hand, she made a motion toward her mouth, asking for something to eat. *No,* he said, and shook his head and looked away. She stood there a few moments longer. Matt Lang tried to focus on his postcards, but she reached out and tapped his forearm. *No,* he said again, this time sliding further away from the window, wondering how this woman got to Mindoro. Did she hitchhike to the port? Did she stow away on the ferry? He watched out of the corner of his eye as she made her way down the beach.

She ran into Brian, once again alone, without Maria. She made the same motion, hand to mouth, asking for food. Matt couldn't hear the conversation, but he saw Brian put his hand on the woman's shoulder and tip his head toward the restaurant. It looked like he said, Come on, then.

Brian and the woman walked into the restaurant. The hostess met them just inside the door.

I'm so sorry ma'am, sir, but the restaurant is for guests staying at the resort only.

The woman looked away. Brian looked at the hostess and said, I know, love, but she'll stay with me, and it's just one meal. The hostess nodded her assent and the two sat down.

Brian ordered their drinks and food. When the drinks came, Brian lifted his bottle towards Matt. Matt lifted his eyebrows and asked, Where's Maria?

Brian took a drink, and made a point of pouring a glass of water for the woman. Matt went back to his postcards, both filled with references to the beauty and hospitality of the country, and the assurances of his safety and well being. He noticed he'd spelled Philippines incorrectly every time, with two l's and one p. He closed his eyes and folded the cards in half and tore them along the fold.

*

Matt convinced Andrea to have breakfast at the restaurant on their last morning at the resort. Brian was sitting at the bar by himself, hair combed as always, two days of scruff on his face. He lifted his bottle when they walked in.

Matt asked again, Where's Maria?

Maria went home, mate. No need to worry about her.

Is she okay?

Brian rapped his knuckles on the bar.

I said she's fine. Don't worry.

Brian looked at Andrea.

How's your book comin'? Matt here told me you were workin' on a book? 'Bout the sex trade, is it? I reckon he thought he was gettin' another chapter for ya.

Brian stood, took a pile of bills from his wallet, dropped them on the bar, and turned to Matt

She was a co-worker, mate. With me 'cause she wanted to be. I'm guilty of having an office romance, nothing more. Her family lives near here, so she went to see them. This country has problems, sure, but I ain't one of 'em.

Matt played detective one more time, looked Brian over for signs of a struggle, some evidence of wrongdoing, a scratch on his neck or cuts on his hands, some marring of his impeccable nails. He didn't see any. A little doubt tugged at his mind, for a beat he thought about apologizing, but he had that same knot in his gut, and his jaw was getting tighter. Brian was wrong, Brian was bad, Matt was right, Matt was good. Matt was certain of these facts. He thought of subduing Brian, calling the police, finding Maria — trapped, bound, hungry, somehow cold and shivering — reuniting her with her family, the tears, the gratitude, the celebration dinner and the celebratory news coverage, the boost that would give to Andrea's book, the book tour and the stories that would lead to more women being found and more reunions, so many wrongs made right.

Andrea grabbed his arm.

Come on. Let's go.

Manila

Manila is less a city than a head-on collision at a five-way intersection, a compelling clusterfuck, a Gordian knot in which twenty million people try to live. The bus crawled past crowded shacks built right up to the edge of the road, barely room enough for a person to stand between the shoulder and the front door, past roadside eateries that were smoky and hot in a city that needed neither of those elements, past men sleeping in rickshaws. *Pressing* was the word that kept going through Matt's head; he had no idea what was happening in Andrea's head. He was certain her head was full of thoughts. He wanted to know those thoughts, but she was sleeping on his shoulder and he didn't want to break the spell. She woke up when the jeepney next to their window sounded its horn for at least a full minute. She sat up and smiled.

It's a mess, but I think I love this city.

Matt wondered how you could love a city that was killing you slowly, smothering you with its own exhaust, but he could tell by the way she leaned on him, the way she held his hand, the softness that had come back to her face, that she was happier here.

I'm glad you're better.

She looked at him like he had just spit in her eye.

What are you talking about?

He'd broken the spell. She let go of his hand, sat up straight, shifted toward the aisle.

I mean, he said, it's nice to see you happy.

But you said *better*.

Better was the wrong word. Better was bitter and bad on her tongue.

Well, better compared to when we were at the resort.

What was wrong with me at the resort?

Matt Lang wished he could turn this car around, but the brakes had been cut and there was nothing left to do but careen down the highway and hope the casualties were few.

You seemed upset.

I seemed upset? Was I not supposed to be upset? You think I should have — what?

I — let's talk about something else.

No. Let's talk about this. You don't have a clue do you?

Apparently not.

The stories I've heard. Women lied to, stolen from, trapped, raped. Trapped and raped and when they're used up they're left out on the street. Do you think for a second that Maria is home with her family? That Maria is even her real name?

Matt looked to see if others on the bus were listening to their conversation. Most people were sleeping or watching the movie playing on the television at the front. Something with Steven Seagal.

No, I don't. Never did. I was on it from the beginning.

You made it worse is what you did. The guy probably got nervous, stuck her in a cab, and sent her to the nearest dock. Maybe he gave her some money to get back to Manila, maybe she had to fuck someone else to get home. You might have cost her her rent for the month, or food for her kids. It's shitty work, but it's not as simple as you coming to the rescue and making everything better.

Matt Lang wondered how better became such a bad word. His arms and head felt heavy. He rubbed his eyes with the heels of his hands. In Erie, he realized, it was late morning. The playground in the park at the end of his street was filling with children. If he was home, he would be reading in his living room with the window open and he'd be able to hear them laughing and playing and he'd think about how nice the world is.

I didn't know.

No, you didn't, and you didn't ask.

I'm sorry.

The bus drove past a line of food carts, each with a small table next to them, two chairs at each table, an old woman at each food cart, fanning at the pots of food to keep the flies away. The bus was so close, and moving so slowly, that Matt could have reached out the window and purchased a plate of food from any one of the women. They looked at him as if they hoped he'd do just that. Inside the bus, Steven Seagal was single-handedly taking on a restaurant full of bad guys.

I'm sorry, too, Andrea said. I'm still trying to figure out what to do with all this. I can help tell the stories — help them tell their own stories — but then what? I go home, package the stories so they'll resonate with Americans, because they always have to resonate with Americans, because America is always the only thing that ever matters, so that means taking great, big issues — she held her hands wide — and turning them into these single issues with individual stories — she shrunk the gap so her palms were inches apart — and trust that it still counts for something. That'll take a year, two years. Then the book comes out and how many people will read it? And what difference will that make?

What does your friend Dora say when you talk about this?

Andrea leaned back into him, and put her hand on his chest.

She talks about bearing witness, about speaking the truth, about trusting the work.

Maybe all the rest is up to — . Matt couldn't find the word, he waved his hand in the air at nothing in particular.

Maybe that's the difference. Dora has faith in this — Andrea matched Matt Lang's gesture — and I don't.

*

It was dark by the time the bus pulled into the terminal at Cubao. They carried their bags around broken concrete, sleeping street children, stray animals, piles of shit, and puddles of liquid that defied taxonomy. As they waited at the gate to get into the compound,

Matt heard the collapse and crinkle of a paper bag and turned to see a woman with spidery hair breathing into it. He saw the mole, and when she looked up from the bag he saw her tongue roll in her mouth as she spoke silent words.

As the watchman opened the gate, the woman lunged and wrapped her arms around Andrea's neck. Matt grabbed the woman, pulled her away, and held her at a distance. In Erie, children were running home to get lunch, and if he were there, he'd be finishing the paragraph he was reading and thinking about lunch of his own.

Just let her go, Andrea said.

He did and she fell on her back. She laughed and rolled on the sidewalk as Matt Lang and Andrea stepped into the compound and the watchman closed the gate behind them.

The Tar Black Road and the Lava Red Moon
(Featuring the Dust Brown Haze)

Pulling out of the parking lot.
   [Idle chitchat about the quality of the meal.]
   Waiting at the red light. Turning left when they see the green arrow.
   Merging onto the interstate.
   His thoughts on her mouth as he looks out the window. He sees a lava red moon on the horizon.
   [Words about the child, how quiet it is without her. Agreement about the fact that it is quiet in the car.]
   Amy Winehouse on the radio.
   Remembering things, thinking too much. He pictures a calendar. He wants the calendar to go away. He tries to concentrate on a silo in the distance, but the silo becomes a one (1) and the counting begins. Dates flip through his mind as if they were papers on a desk, blown away by wind through an open window.
   His eyes now on her. She is driving with hands at ten and two. She is looking straight ahead. Does she know he is looking at her? He doesn't think so. What is she thinking about? He doesn't want to know. She is probably thinking about the tar black road underneath the tires, while he is thinking about the lava red moon.
   A commercial on the radio. Another commercial.
   [A suggestion by him that they turn to another station, previously enjoyed by both of them, a dismissal by her of his suggestion, a dispute about the radio, something about the presets, his confusion, an attempt to clarify, an okay, fine.]
   An unbelievable amount of flat farmland.
   [His comment about his sore shoulder.]
   Her silent attention on the tar black road.
   Eric Clapton on the radio.
   His thoughts again on her mouth, how it is tense when he kisses her, he tries to remember when this started. A billboard that says no man shall know the date and time. Each billboard looks like a square on a calendar. Dates and times, things to come, days gone by.

His eyes back on her. He wants to talk about the lava red moon.
[Look at the lava red moon.]
[I'm trying to watch the road.]
Further thoughts about the moon kept to himself.
[Another comment about his shoulder, her observation that he is just falling apart, isn't he.]

Closer to the city. More billboards. He closes his eyes to shut out the dates. Now there are dates on the inside of his eyelids. He hates his brain, the way it keeps track of events, and marks them on a calendar, and constantly measures the distance from one to another.

A commercial on the radio.

His reclines his seat, touching the empty car seat behind him. He sits the seat back up. His eyes are open again. There's a dust brown haze between the road and the moon. The city lights are blurry. It was a dry summer, so little rain.

[A disagreement about what exit to take. Her first mention of the lava red moon that has been there all along.]

First appeared as the liner notes to the album *Very Close to Strangers* by Matthew Black, released in May 2013. Listen to him at matthewblackmusic.com

Six Words, Six Stories

Stolen

There's sleet hitting my window. It's 6:38 in the morning. The alarm is set for 6:45, but I guess I'll get up and make tea.

The first step of the day is the hardest. When I was twenty, I did the Appalachian Trail in a summer. Ultra light, I ran much of it. Now my knees threaten to give out on the way down the hall to the bathroom. It takes all morning to untie the knot in my back, which could snap with a cough or a sneeze. My shoulders are painful connections. It hurts when I lift my arms to wash my face. I have Plantar's Fasciitis in my left foot. But my heart is well, and free.

I pull my robe tight across my chest with one hand and light the stove with the other. As the water warms towards boiling, I go to check the mail, which I didn't check yesterday.

Once a year, for the past twenty-five years, I have received a postcard from a different part of the world. The first was from Burlington, Vermont, another was from Gibraltar, still another from Auckland, with others from points in between. This one is from India.

The early sun is fighting its way through the clouds and sleet. I sink into the chair near my front window. Some of the outside air is sneaking in. I'm grateful for my robe.

On the front is a picture of my heart (they all have pictures of my heart, how she makes these postcards, I don't know) in front of the Taj Mahal. She is not always in the picture, but in this I see her red hair is now gray. She looks twenty pounds leaner than she was the day she left, with muscles I don't remember, but which must have been there all along, underneath everything. She is in the foreground, the Taj Mahal in the distance, and a reflecting pool is in between. The perspective is such that it looks like she is taller than the building. She is holding my heart in the air, above the dome, and, in two dimensions, it looks as if it, my heart, could either balance, if she chose to let it go, or get pierced on the tip of the spire. The look on her face hints that she is contemplating the possibilities. But they're just thoughts, she won't let it go, she will pack my heart away and carry it to the next place.

I hear a whistle. The water must be ready.

SKY

HE IS one hundred feet from his front door, almost to the sidewalk. He is wearing grey trousers and a black wool overcoat, which is buttoned to fight the cold, with help from a scarf, which is also grey. Underneath the coat he's wearing a light blue shirt with the top button undone, bits of the collar peaking from under the scarf, two wedges of sky on an otherwise overcast outfit. He has on his nicest shoes, which he shined earlier in the day. His hair is slicked tight against his head, parted and combed from right to left. His face is thin and clean-shaven. He is wearing black gloves. He is standing completely still.

Five minutes before he left his house, he hung up the phone. Five minutes before he hung up the phone, he listened to what was said to him. Before he listened, he took five minutes to say what he'd meant to say, and five minutes before he said what he'd meant to say, he took a drink, combed his hair and reached for the phone.

A neighbor sits in her living room across the street and watches him. His feet are slightly more than shoulder width apart as he stands there near the sidewalk. It seems, to her, an unnatural way to stand. She wonders what he is doing, where he might be going, as she watches him slick his hair down with his right hand. She is worried but not sure why. She wants to keep her eye on him, but now her view is blocked by a moving van heading west.

A cat lies on her lap and wonders and worries about nothing as she scratches it behind the ears.

Inside his house, all the dishes are washed, dried and put away. His bed is made. All the lights are off. The thermostat is turned down to an efficient 64 degrees. The rooms are vacuumed, even under the sofas and desks and bookshelves. The backdoor is locked. The front door, to make this one thing easier for his friends and family, he has left unlocked. They will find a note on his laptop, in the middle of his dining room table next to his phone, wallet, keys, and relevant papers.

Falling

OL' JACK he had a plan, he said, to paint the town he lived in red. He'd take the place by storm, by God! But first he needed water.

To fetch the drink, he'd need a hand; it's not a job for just a man. It takes two strong, brave, beating hearts to get the sought-for water.

So Jack got on the telephone, and he called Jill, she was at home. "Jill, come with me, and bring your pail. Why? To fetch some water."

Fair Jill, she liked his way with words, his eyes when he would look at her. "Jack, I've got my pail right here. It's ready for the water."

They both met up at the bottom of the hill where the grass was green and the air was still. Side by side they stood there tall and looked at the top of the hill and all they thought about was life and how it was going to change.

"Jill, you never looked so grand, I am a goddamn lucky man to have you hold my steady hand. We are going to change this town or burn the fucker to the ground with the friction of our efforts. Today is today. It will end with today. Tomorrow will last forever."

"Jack, you handsome, toothy bastard, this place is made of glass and plaster, the two of us could never last here. You and I are young and free, sunlight carried by a breeze that always finds the window. We'll climb up this hill, drop our pail in the well, then pull it back up together."

Now we can see young Jack and Jill, standing there on top of the hill. The houses wait below their feet. Their pail is full of water.

We know of course that Jack will fall, tumble down like an egg-shaped ball. His head will find a patient rock. The sound will fill the valley.

Jill's feet will also let her down, she'll roll along the sloping ground, and when she stops, she'll hold the pail. The pail will hold no water.

But as for now they're side by side, so let them think today has died. They've almost raised the pail back up. Can almost taste the water.

STARS

Ras Algethi

When you were seventeen, Ras saw you drop acid and try to go fishing in the pond on the edge of town. Ras twinkled just above the trees on the far side of the pond while you, Shane and Clark laughed and cried as you tried to cast your bait into the sky.

"I can catch them," you insisted, "because the stars are like fish in the pond of the air. They don't twinkle, they don't twinkle, look closer, they ripple. That's water." You'd cast the bait high into the sky, only to watch it come down with a plop.

Yed Prior

Yed was there when you were twenty-one and you sat next to Megan Hourigan on the porch at your Uncle George's cottage. You might not have seen him, he was kind of behind you, but he watched you creep your hand toward her as she told you about her mother's last visit to the doctor.

You! Here was a twenty-year-old girl who was about to lose her mother and you saw it as a chance to get laid.

You! You put your arm around her shoulder and you reached under her shirt. Yed saw you!

You. You pulled away. You weren't like that you said to yourself, with thoughts that Yed could hear.

She. She wished you hadn't stopped.

Alrakis

In your thirties, you had a thing for hookers. It's cool. Alrakis never judged you. She didn't even judge you when she saw you pulled over on the side of the road, screaming into your cell phone, wiping your nose with the back of your rolled-up sleeve, begging Fred to help you make this go away, as your high-priced companion hemorrhaged in the passenger seat of your Mazda Miata.

Fred came through, he was good like that. Only he and Alrakis know the truth.

Chort

Chort shined on you off the coast of St. Thomas while you and your third wife took a honeymoon cruise. Do you remember meeting the couple from South Africa? Yes. The four of you had dinner together on the second night. By the time Chort took notice, it was clear your wife was going to sleep with the two of them while you kneeled by the toilet, felled by seasickness and an open bar. This marriage would last three weeks.

You should have asked Chort, she of the heavenly perspective. She would have told you about what had been and what would be. She could see beyond the horizon and was unaffected by the waves.

Hydrobius

On your last night on earth, Hydrobius alone was visible through the clouds and city lights. He had such high hopes for you, and it broke his celestial heart to see you broken in the alley. He worried when you stepped onto the railing of the balcony and tried to jump to the next balcony over. You should not have gone out on the balcony, you should have answered the door and gone with the officers. For insider trading you would have done five years, less with good behavior.

What made you think you could make such a jump? It must have been fifteen feet to that other balcony. And it had rained!

Poor Hydrobius, he loved you so much and all he could do was watch you leap and fall. He yelled, but he was so far away, and sound travels so slowly, that his warning was too late.

High

HISTORY WAS made on the night the supervisors of Duncan Township voted to build the highest high dive in Dayton County, and in so doing finally stick it to the supervisors and residents of Smithfield Township, who thought they were so great. The vote was 6-1. To pay for the high dive, they voted to close the library and sell the fire department's lone fire truck. Volunteers, using their own trucks and their own hoses, would fight any future fires. The residents of Duncan were thrilled.

The high dive was supposed to be forty-five feet high. That's high! But after the fire truck brought in less money than expected, the plans were scaled back to thirty-five. Still high! It was completed in time for summer, and a driver driving along Route 77 could see it poke above the pool house. The whole county was talking about it, and people from as far away as Ricksburg came for the grand opening.

The high school marching band played, a veteran of a foreign war spoke, and then Robert Drinkwalter climbed the ladder and walked to the edge of the board. Robert was chosen for the inaugural leap because he was retarded and therefore inspirational. He jumped from the board, smacked the water, and sank like a stone. The quarterback of the football team, Jeremy Burrows, swam him to safety and the gathered citizens applauded politely as Robert twitched and coughed near the gutter. The local priest, Father Michael Thyme, offered a closing prayer before dismissing the crowd. Even the few residents of Smithfield Township who had come to cast a wary eye on the proceedings had to admit it was something.

In fact, Smithfield Township had no choice but to come up with its own plan for a higher high dive, paid for by eliminating all parks, all schools, all libraries and any and all public safety providers. It was unveiled at a ceremony in which returning vets executed an accused pornographer and the official first jump was made by Tammy Henderson, a child so disabled that she had to be raised up in a basket and thrown from the board by her sister, Tabitha. Pastor Steven Cash, a Baptist with a lovely wife and two darling boys delivered the closing prayer. Grown men wept, mothers kissed their daughters on their foreheads.

Years from now, the occasional tourist will stop to see the high dives that they read about on billboard after billboard after billboard. These tourists might pull their cars or vans over and get out and get their picture taken. Or not. They might buy a snow globe or some postcards. Who knows? Some may choose to have a drink at the High Dive Bar and Grill where the beer will be cheap and they might meet Quarterback Jeremy Burrows. He will drink there most days. Whatever they do, these tourists will all remark, to themselves or out loud, not so much about the high dives in Duncan or Smithfield, but about the dazzling sunsets, the result, some will say, of all the large fires that burn across Dayton County.

Flying

I REMEMBER riding in a boat on the South China Sea. Beautiful day, that day was. There were just a few clouds in the sky and the water was flat, like a big-ass turquoise tabletop. Seven of us were skim, skim, skimming over the surface of the ocean and every few minutes I would belt out, *"Her name is Rio/and she dances on the sand!"* My friends grew tired of this, but our guide, Don-Don, kept saying, "Oh, you are a singer. That's good." Don-Don knew what he was talking about.

Out in the ocean, far from land, we saw flying fish. *Flying* fish. That's some shit. And we saw many flying fish. If you've never seen flying fish do their thing, know this: they glitter. On days when the sun is high and the clouds are gone, when they arc from Ocean Point A to Ocean Point B, they glitter and glisten like crystals.

Some of these fish could make it over the boat. Think of it: you're sitting there in a motorboat with six other people, you're skipping over the ocean and a sparkly fish flies past your face. Life is amazing, I tell you.

One fish didn't quite make it. It left the water and landed in the middle of our boat. Don-Don grabbed it by the tail, bashed its head on the railing, and stashed it in a small Styrofoam cooler with his San Miguel beer.

There were two groups on the boat. There were those who thought the fish should have known better, who said that this is what happens when fish try to fly, who felt that flying was only meant for birds, insects and creatures that can build airplanes; and there were the rest of us who loved the fish for trying

Acknowledgements

Thank you to Jason Cashing, Herman Aguirre, Marlene Lang, Michael Lang, and all my other patrons. To support me via *Patreon*, go to www.patreon.com/mattlang.

A big thank you and tip of the hat to David Feaman for his artwork on the "Opal Room". He made my words jump in surprising ways. His talent elevates this whole collection.

Thank you to Amelia Lorenz, Emily Hendel, Greg Boettner, Jesse Larson, Katie Rains, Matthew Black and Shawna Bowman for reading different drafts of different stories and giving honest feedback.

Particular thanks goes to Matthew Black for asking me to write stories to go along with his album. Such trust.

Thank you to Eric Westerlind for his careful edits of many of these stories, and for his all-around support and enthusiasm for the words I write.

Amelia Lorenz's vivid descriptions of Panther Hollow in Pittsburgh inspired "Skipping Stones". A more generous author would give her some sort of official credit as a co-writer, but, alas, I'm a scoundrel.

Emily Hendel gave me the prompt that became "A Hot Dog Love Story", and her love and support daily give me joy and rest. All these stories would be unfinished without her.

About the Author

Matt Lang was born in Olean, New York and lived there for one year before moving with his family up and over the hill, across the border, to Rixford, Pennsylvania, into the house in which his mother grew up.

He went to college in Erie, Pennsylvania, and lived there for two years in an almost constant state of misery. Had he stayed, he would have written one indispensable piece of American fiction before freezing to death surrounded by empty bottles in the abandoned house in which he would have been squatting. But he left.

He transferred to the College of Wooster and was happy there. He met the most important people in his life, including Emily Hendel, now his wife.

Now he lives in a large house on the Southwest Side with his wife, daughter, and others, including some of those same important people from Wooster. He's written American fiction, including *Fernweh*, *McKean County and Other Stories*, and *The Giraffe's Mustache: A Storybook You Can Color*, the indispensability of which are debatable, but his house is well heated, if, at times, drafty.

*This book was typeset in 10pt Cardo,
a free, strangely lovely Google font.*

*Cover and interior design is by
Alyssa Bozekowski & Eric Westerlind*

CPSIA information can be obtained
at www.ICGtesting.com
Printed in the USA
FFOW02n0251150216
21477FF